"I've h
here with y

Rafe drew a hand across his throat. "You've been sniping at me from the time we met. It's got to stop!" He crashed a fist into the trunk of the tree, and Ziggy's eyes widened in alarm.

"Not for my sake," he continued, "but for the sake of your grandfather. Lord knows why, but he already thinks the sun rises and sets with you. And I don't want to see him hurt."

Ziggy's eyes flickered with fury as he went on. "So why don't you do as your father and uncle did, deny your responsibilities and get the hell back where you came from!"

"You'd like that wouldn't you?" Ziggy flashed, anger making her stomach churn. "I walk away, so Gramps disinherits me and you stand to come into everything. Very neat!"

And in the dense silent woodland, seeing the volcanic expression on Rafe's face, she felt afraid for the first time in her life.

Diana Hamilton creates high-tension conflict that brings new life to traditional romance. Readers find her a welcome addition to the Harlequin Romance line and will be glad to know that more novels by this talented author are already in the works.

Painted Lady

Diana Hamilton

Harlequin Books

TORONTO • NEW YORK • LONDON
AMSTERDAM • PARIS • SYDNEY • HAMBURG
STOCKHOLM • ATHENS • TOKYO • MILAN

Original hardcover edition published in 1988
by Mills & Boon Limited

ISBN 0-373-02959-4

Harlequin Romance first edition February 1989

CHAPTER ONE

ZIGGY BELLINGHAM moved gracefully within the pre-
scribed confines of the troupe's patch, the bright sunlight highlighting the matt white greasepaint that covered
her face and neck, artfully sculpting the delicate
moulding of her classical facial bone-structure while the
heavy black lines limning her eyes emphasised the gamine
slant, the deep and almost startlingly vivid azure of her
irises.

The stark white leotard she wore clipped her tall, rangy
body lovingly from neck to ankle as she moved through
her robotic dance sequence with an effortless and athletic precision, every muscle controlled, the movements
dramatic but containing an underlying subtlety that
added a new dimension, something difficult to pin down
and impossible to define.

The warmth of the early May sun had tempted many
strollers and shoppers to the open-air tables that spilled
out from the small cafés and restaurants of the Covent
Garden piazza and a crowd had gathered to watch, the
usual, or so she supposed. Her mind was on other things.
Mundane things—what to cook for supper tonight, it
was her turn to feed the troupe. Momentous things—
what to do with her future since she had no wish to stay
with the troupe for ever. A week, to Ziggy, sometimes
seemed like for ever.

Performing, she rarely saw the crowd as a collection
of individuals, real people. She was aware of them, of
course she was, but only as a mass—students filtering

down from the open-air stalls of the market, yuppies—
the trendy young upwardly mobiles who percolated
through from the classy shops and boutiques in the
piazza—a few derelicts scavenging among the tables.

But today there was one onlooker she couldn't fail to
notice. Whoever he was, he would never surrender his
identity to any crowd. He held himself apart, his
aloofness diminishing the others, pushing them back
beyond the barriers of existence, making her aware of
him. Only of him. His presence reached out to her, she
could almost feel it. And she didn't like it.

The music ended as Ziggy's lissome young body arched
into a backward-bending bow, athletic and beautiful,
holding every eye, and the other three members of the
troupe moved forward, surrounding her, two of them
going into the mime while the third, Sam, in his scarlet
and black harlequin suit, wove around the edge of the
crowd with the collecting box, bowing elaborately and
rattling his tambourine whenever a monetary offering
was made, keeping the smile on his face even when a
supercilious young trendy drawled, 'Get lost, guy—work
for a living, why don't you?'

Ziggy slid into the background, releasing her white
bandeau and allowing her waist-length wealth of water-
straight black hair to fall free. Her back turned to the
crowd, she clipped a shocking pink crinoline around the
neat span of her waist, crammed a huge poke bonnet
on her head, added a quick smear of vivid lipstick,
making an exaggerated cupid's bow, and was ready to
clown with the others.

Damien and Kate were miming the parts of eighteenth-century rakes-around-town, Ziggy the pursued and
rather lunatic young maiden, and she unwillingly caught
the eyes of the man in the crowd, met his level, pen-

etrating grey stare yet again, and warning bells jangled in her brain.

At first she had thought that sheer good looks alone—allied to impeccable tailoring—set him apart, made him noticeable. You didn't often get the urbane, sophisticated tycoon-type here, not watching the antics of the street entertainers, you didn't. But it was more than mere good looks and expensive packaging that set him apart. It was the look in his eyes. Intent, watching her, only her, not the others. The other performers might not have existed. The eyes of the crowds were never that intent, that knowing. Interested, yes—if they hung around long enough to watch—amused and relaxed. Never cold and minutely watchful. It was as if he knew her from somewhere. Which he didn't.

Ziggy, twirling between Damien and Kate to a strident chord from Sam's harmonica, squashed the idea of an eagle-eyed talent scout with an inner giggle that almost succeeded in banishing her uneasy wariness. She was good, but nowhere near that good. And he was no talent scout.

A clash of cymbals—Sam again—cued her into a low, flowing curtsey, and after holding it for seconds while Sam took up the collecting box again she raised her head. The ridiculous bonnet wavered and she found her eyes travelling up the length of long immaculately trousered legs, skimming the breadth of a superbly cut lovat suit jacket and on to a tanned, proudly authoritative face, the hard, assertive lines of boldly drawn cheekbones, the glittering mockery of slate-grey eyes, the cruelly passionate curve of a shockingly beautiful, sensual male mouth.

The impact of that look shook her, and Ziggy didn't shake easily. Canadian, twenty years old and free as a bird as she was, no one had yet succeeded in putting her down. Yet the stranger looked as though he could, no hassle. And would, given half a chance.

With more reasons than one to be thankful, she re- alised it was time for a ten-minute break. Ziggy tried to put the man out of her mind as she reached for four cans of Coke from her duffle bag, handing them round, sticking close to her friends, using them as a safety barrier because although the crowd was drifting away she knew darned well he wasn't.

Sensing his approach through every minute nerve- ending, she stiffened and resisted the vapid impulse to cling on to someone, anyone, because she wasn't a girl who clung. She stood her own ground, always had done, and that was something she'd inherited from her English- born father, certainly not from her Canadian mother, whose name should have been Ivy!

'Miss Bellingham? Ziggy Bellingham, of Gibsons Landing, British Columbia?' The clipped, well-educated accent, suggesting the hallowed precincts of the cream of English public schools, was precisely the sound she had known that mouth would produce. She bristled in- stinctively, immediate antagonism devastating her with its unaccustomed savagery, heating her blood. She turned slowly to face him, staring impassively from slanting azure eyes, resisting the impulse to snarl because that would be a dead give-away. She didn't want him to know he had got to her, that his use of her name had made her more than uneasy.

'Rafe d'Anjou.' He offered a slip of white paste- board, not his hand. The look in his eyes, the curve of his mouth, told her he'd walk a mile rather than touch her, and Ziggy, childishly, thrust her hands behind her back, refusing to take his card. How did a guy who looked and sounded like a member of the tradition-bound British upper classes get a Gallic-sounding handle like that? Come to think of it, though—azure eyes narrowed consideringly beneath a fringe of heavy black lashes, the dark limning giving their slanting line an extra inscrutability—there was something Latin about his aura of potent, unthinking masculine dominance, about the sable hair, the straight and haughty line of nose and cheekbone.

'May I present Arthur Greaves, private investigator, Miss Bellingham.' He was introducing his companion, smallish, stoutish, baldish. Ziggy hadn't noticed him in the crowd. But then she wouldn't have, would she? Not when this Rafe Whatever had staked his silent claim to her undivided yet reluctant attention.

Kate giggled nervously, just behind her, and Damien said, in his rough brown voice, 'Been robbing a bank, darling?' and Ziggy shivered, unaccountably and suddenly cold.

She felt her friends move round her protectively and she was grateful for that, grateful, too, for the disguise of her white-painted face, black-rimmed eyes—even for the stupid scarlet cupid's bow of her painted mouth. Arthur Greaves said quickly, placatingly, 'There's nothing to be alarmed about, Miss Bellingham. My client——'

'Would like a word. In private,' Rafe d'Anjou cut in, his voice chillingly decisive. 'It concerns your grandfather.'

She felt the uncomfortable trickle of sweat down her back, and the effort of lifting one eyebrow in a parody of nonchalance was more difficult than she would have believed possible. 'Anything you have to say can be said in front of my friends. Only make it snappy, we're trying to earn a living.'

She turned her back on him, removing the absurd poke bonnet, and calmly re-secured her hair beneath the wide white bandeau. She was being deliberately rude. It was out of character, but better that than allow him to see how the mention of her grandfather had upset her. A gut reaction, she supposed, something in her roots. Her English grandfather was a topic her mother brought out secretly, as often as she could. When her father had been alive he wouldn't have the old man's name mentioned.

'I prefer to speak to you alone. What time do you finish here?'

His voice grated on her nerves; that tone, that inflection, was something her father had been known to mimic savagely when, on the rare occasions when he'd had too much to drink, he had dropped his acquired Canadian drawl. And Damien's, 'Another couple of hours at least,' annoyed her too. She hated it when other people took it upon themselves to answer for her—the man had been speaking to her, dammit! And the clipped comeback, 'I can't afford to hang around that long, my time's valuable,' uttered in a tone of impatient disgust, set her skin burning hotly beneath the thick white layer of greasepaint.

'So is ours,' Damien pointed out, his dark brown eyes satisfied as Rafe d'Anjou got the message, removing a soft leather wallet from an inner pocket and extracting four crisp brown notes.

Damien handed the money to Sam and started to strip off his elaborate wig, his velvet frock coat, and Ziggy fumed. The arrogant bastard had bought their time, and as far as the others were concerned he had bought her too!

Well, Ziggy Bellingham wasn't up for grabs, and when the nondescript private investigator offered, gesturing, 'There's a vacant table just there, maybe the three of us can sit and talk, Miss Bellingham?' she lifted a pointed painted chin, her North American drawl as insultingly laid back as she could make it.

'Thanks, but no, thanks. If anyone wants to talk to me——' she deliberately did not look at the disturbing d'Anjou character '—then I can spare about ten minutes of my time around seven this evening. At my place. Get that? I guess you have the address, learning that would have come well within your brief.'

She swung away, towards her gear, knowing she'd won this round. D'Anjou would not be pleased; his type expected to win, always, to deal with losers all along the line. And she was no loser. But although the thought pleased her, she knew that it would make their 'talk' this evening that much more difficult—to say the very least!

It was the part of the day Ziggy disliked most. Tubing it back to Bethnal Green, she always felt tacky. Jeans and a shirt covered her leotard, making her feel uncomfortable, and the imperfectly cleaned-off white greasepaint earned her a few odd looks. And today, after d'Anjou had handed out that money, Kate and Sam had sloped off somewhere, presumably to spend their share, and she and Damien were having to tote the extra gear.

She ignored Damien sprawled out on the seat beside her, she didn't want to have to talk to anyone right now. She must have been off her head to insist that the d'Anjou character call to see her. She should have swallowed her pride and done what the private investigator had suggested, sat down, had a coffee or something and listened politely to whatever it was they had wanted to say. And that would have been the end of it.

Instead, wanting to be the one to call the tune, reverse the insufferable creature's impression that he could buy her time, her attention, she had insisted that he drop by the rooming house where she shared her space with the troupe. And that was something she wasn't eagerly anticipating!

Whatever it was he had to say to her had something to do with her grandfather, he'd made that much clear. Was the old guy dead, or something? Had he left her something in his will? Mom had said that she thought he was fairly well heeled—an impression gained from something Dad had once said, apparently. And if that were the case Ziggy would refuse to take it, whatever it was. And how had the d'Anjou guy and the investigator tracked her down? As far as she knew, Grandfather Bellingham hadn't even known that his runaway son had married, let alone produced a child.

She sighed, squirming in her seat because she felt hot and uncomfortable and oddly restless. Meeting up with the troupe had been one of the good things life sometimes carelessly tossed at the feet of those with the wits to take advantage of such offerings. Recently come on a visit to England, she had been living as cheaply as she could in a shabby boarding house near Euston Station, seeing the sights of London on a shoestring. Moving in with the troupe, finding a niche for herself in the two rooms and kitchen they rented in Bethnal Green, taking her share of their earnings, had eked out her small amount of spending money. It was the first time she had ever had reason to be grateful for her mother's insistence that she take dance and deportment classes whenever they had lived long enough in a locality that offered such amenities.

*   *   *

It began to rain as they emerged from the tube station and Damien grumbled dourly, 'This I could do without!' He was lugging Sam's gear as well as his own but, as Ziggy was similarly burdened with Kate's stuff and was being rained on just as heavily, she didn't see the need to offer sympathy.

Damien was a drop-out from drama college, and forming the troupe, a year ago, had been his idea. Ziggy had never done anything like it before, but she was outgoing and game for anything and had found it fun. Besides, it paid her share of the rent and housekeeping, and she got on well with the others, particularly Kate and Sam who shared the only bedroom because they were a couple. They had both been unemployed since leaving school four years ago but were doing their best to make a living, pulling themselves up by their bootstraps. Ziggy admired them, they were her kind of people. Dad would have liked them too, but her mother would have been horrified, so in her sketchy letters to that lady she hadn't mentioned what she was doing. There was no point in upsetting her.

Damien could sometimes be a pain, but Ziggy would always be grateful to him for absorbing her into the life of the troupe. Her five weeks with them had helped her over the depression that had clung following her father's death. So she tried to cheer him up, reminding him,

'You can put your feet up this evening. It's my turn to make supper, Sam's to clear up after.'

They believed in an equal division of labour, of the profits—if any—after the bills had been paid. Individual equality was something Ziggy passionately believed in, as her father had done, and Damien only got stroppy when he thought his authority was being undermined. As now. Though why he should think he had

any right to authority, when all were supposedly equal,
was something Ziggy couldn't make out. She was going
to have to tackle him about it, if she stayed with them.
And this resolve was strengthened as the reason for his
bad mood became clear.

'Why did you have to invite that guy round? You could
have listened to what the jerk had to say there and then.
You knew I'd earmarked this evening to talk through
the new mime routine I've been working on.'

Trudging at his side, Ziggy snapped,

'I pay my share of the rent, so I guess I can invite a
visitor now and then! Besides, I don't like feeling I've
been bought. That arrogant swine thought he only had
to wave a few tenners around to get us peasants grovel-
ling at his feet. Nobody buys me, or my time, and you
should have thrown his money back at him!'

'Prickly, aren't you?' Damien turned the corner and
Ziggy trundled after him, clutching at the various bags
and boxes that were threatening to slither out of her
arms.

Prickly? She'd been called that before. By her mother.
But her father had referred to her self-determination as
'A fine streak of independence—a real chip off the old
block!' and that was good enough for her.

Luckily there was some hot water and the bathroom they
shared with the tenants from the rooms below had been
left reasonably clean. Ziggy lay in the chipped bathtub
and wondered if Rafe d'Anjou would be on time,
whether he'd bother to turn up at all. She didn't much
care, either way. She had no idea who he was or why
he, or her grandfather, had hired an investigator to track
her to BC and from there back to England. She wasn't
interested, and if he showed up she would tell him so.

Stepping out of the tub at last, she dried herself briskly, enjoying the sensation of feeling clean and fresh again, and wondered just what it was about the d'Anjou character that got her on the raw. Even before he'd mentioned her grandfather she had instinctively disliked him. Or disliked what he stood for. Over-privilege, the unmistakable aura of superiority, were things she had no time for. No time at all. And that accent, the way he'd handed over forty pounds as if it were forty pence, had set her hackles rising.

Ziggy had an ingrained sense of her own worth as an individual who was equal to, and no better than, the billions of other individuals who inhabited this planet. She knew her rights as such because her father had instilled them into her almost since birth, but she wasn't aggressive about it. She was fairly even-tempered, philosophical—well, most of the time. That man brought out the very worst in her.

She dressed again, her fresh jeans fitting her long lithe legs and neat hips snugly, her T-shirt skimming her high round breasts with a decorum that owed itself to the fact that the garment was several sizes too large and had been borrowed from Sam because everything she owned, apart from the fresh jeans, had needed washing. She would go to the launderette after that man left, if he ever arrived. He might have given up on her, thrown in the towel. She hoped he had, but he didn't seem the type.

The others had drifted off to the pub to discuss the new mime routine and celebrate the unlooked-for forty pounds bonus, leaving the field clear for Ziggy to entertain her visitor.

'Unless you want us here for protection?' Kate had asked quite seriously, but Ziggy had grinned, shooing them out of the door. 'I can handle him. If you're still in the pub when I get back from the launderette, I'll join you,' she'd promised. 'The guy's getting ten minutes, if he shows at all. He didn't look the type to be seen dead in this street.'

They were more curious than she to discover what it was all about, Ziggy admitted as she looked round the living area with mingled disgust and amusement. She wondered if she had time to tidy up, then decided against it. It would take a firm of interior designers a couple of weeks to get this place looking any better than a run-down clutter of broken old junk shop furniture, threadbare rugs and plain tat.

She was rather looking forward to seeing Mr Savile Row Suit in these surroundings! Couldn't wait to see his expression when he came face to face, probably for the first time in his over-protected life, with the way the other half lived!

An imperious double ring on the doorbell one flight down alerted her to his arrival. No one rang the bell, they just walked in and up. Without quite knowing why, Ziggy paused in front of the disintegrating mirror before going down to let him in. She looked composed enough, though she certainly wasn't feeling it. Her hair was tied back into her nape, making her neck look slender and almost childishly vulnerable. Pity about that. But her lips were clamped into an uncompromising line. No simpering, helpless female, this, the slanting eyes confirmed, but a self-possessed, cool young woman who got pushed around by no one.

The expression in the slate-grey eyes was the same—arrogance tinged with a veiling of distaste—but he had changed his suit. Dark grey this time, fitting as impeccably as the lovat had done. Nice for some, Ziggy thought, acknowledging him with a stony expression,

turning quickly and leading the way up the steep flight
of dingy, linoleum-covered stairs.

She took the stairs quickly. She was used to them, was
fit and athletic and could give him at least ten years.
But if she'd hoped he would arrive at the top out of
breath and purple in the face then she was to be
disappointed.

He was right behind her as she pushed on the flaking
brown paint of the door to the rooms she shared, his
breathing not quickened by a fraction. He looked as fit
and hard and tough as they came, she admitted sourly
to herself, recognising the lean strength of the man beneath a suit that, in terms of purchase price, would have
kept her in food and lodging for twelve months.

A lift of one strongly marked brow told her exactly
what he thought of the surroundings, but he wasn't above
sitting when she gestured to one of the armchairs—the
shabbiest in the room. As Ziggy took a chair opposite
him, curling her endless legs under her and cupping her
pointed chin in a long-fingered slim hand, she felt her
heart begin to pound with uncomfortable speed. There
was a chemistry between them that made her dislike him
on sight, and further acquaintance wasn't improving the
situation. Not for him either, she judged, her mouth
compressing against the tight feeling in her throat. He
looked as though the last place on earth he wanted to
be was here, and herself the last person he wanted to be
with.

He leaned forward, his finely made hands hanging
loosely between his grey-clad knees. Fine hands, strong
but well made and immaculately cared for. Square nails,
cut short, new-baby clean. Vividly, Ziggy recalled her
father's hands, the calluses, the broken nails acquired
the hard way, and her exquisitely curved upper lip curled

in derision. This man had probably never done a hard day's work in his life.

He had been watching her closely, his gaze moving over the classical purity of her features, the glint of blue in the raven darkness of the glossy hair that was too savagely scraped back, the thoroughbred lines of the supple young body that even the drab uniformity of the inevitable jeans and T-shirt could not detract from, and Ziggy met his coolly assessing eyes, eyes that communicated nothing, and knew she couldn't stand the unnerving silence any longer.

'Well?'

His mouth curved slightly, the tiniest contraction of the lines fanning out from the eyes that said nothing softening his face a touch. He looked almost human, Ziggy realised, almost regretting the stark belligerence of the single word she had flung at him.

He leaned back in the chair, the harsh but beautifully crafted lines of his face telling her nothing except that, his scrutiny over, he had formed opinions he intended to keep to himself. Not that she cared a rap for his opinions, of course, she didn't believe he had a right to them in any case, and she was about to follow her terse monosyllable with an even terser request that he get to the point, if there was one, when he spoke, pushing the heated words back into her throat where they solidified, emerging at last as a disbelieving grunt when he told her,

'I'm here on behalf of your paternal grandfather, Dudley Bellingham, tenth Earl of Staineswick.'

CHAPTER TWO

'YOU have got to be joking!' Ziggy ground out at last, her voice hoarse, the words dropping slowly, paced out into the silence that had followed his bombshell. Her skin was drained of colour, dewed with sweat across the bridge of her straight neat nose, and her eyes had deepened to sapphire. 'You're out of your skull!'

But she knew the man was serious, sane and serious. Knew it despite the flicker of sardonic amusement that lurked in the grey depths of his eyes, knew it before he reached in an inner pocket and produced two slim white envelopes.

He held them out to her and her eyes were puzzled as she reached out to take them, while he leant back in his chair and steepled his fingers, the look he gave her telling her nothing of what went on inside his head.

'The one is a copy of your father's birth certificate— the Honourable Edward Bellingham who, on his older brother's death, became Viscount Bellingham. The other is a letter from Lord Staineswick, your grandfather. He would like to see you.'

Would he hell! Ziggy thought inelegantly, her mind twisting round in ever-decreasing circles until only one thought was left in uneasy occupation—Viscount Bellingham, her *father*! It was almost laughable. Her grandfather an *earl*, for goodness' sake!

A sudden burden of unshed tears stung her eyes and her throat constricted so that it was difficult to speak, but she managed, huskily.

'Does he—my grandfather—know about Dad?' But he couldn't know, of course he couldn't. The old man hadn't tried to contact his absent son in all those years. There had been a quarrel and Dad had been driven away. 'He died, about eight weeks ago.' It was difficult to say, even now, but she stated shakily, 'It was a logging accident. So you can tell him he's too late. Thirty years too late,' she ended bitterly.

'He knows.' If his voice was milder, gentler, Ziggy was in no emotional state to appreciate it, but his softly put addendum, 'That's why he's so anxious to see you,' got her on the raw, and she swallowed tears and snapped right back,

'Big deal! But maybe I don't want to see him. Has he thought about that?' She twisted the unopened envelopes between tense fingers and rapped out haughtily, 'Dad went to Canada when he was twenty and severed all connections back here. He didn't want to know—he couldn't even bring himself to talk about his English relatives. And I'm my father's daughter,' she added proudly, 'and if his *exalted* family didn't interest him then it doesn't interest me, either!'

'Have you ever stopped to wonder why your father cut himself off so completely?' Rafe d'Anjou countered. His cool eyes pinned her down with something that looked like derision, and Ziggy's stomach squirmed. He was talking about her father. She had idolised him, and this suave, superior *nothing* was talking as though the greatest guy she had ever known was being put on trial, or something. Controlling her resentful anger with difficulty, she came back cuttingly,

'Whatever his reasons for cutting his father out of his life, they would have been good ones. He was a loving man, a family man, so it wouldn't have been youthful thoughtlessness that sent him out to Canada without a backward thought or look. I suggest you ask the *venerable* Earl why he drove his son away!' Her voice was shaking and she drew in a ragged breath. Dad had been the best there was, and she had modelled herself upon him, admiring his independence, the quiet strength that had enabled him to cope with long periods of hard and often lonely work in the great timber forests of Northern British Columbia. And he'd handled the disillusionment of seeing the pretty young Canadian girl he'd married turn into a complaining shrew with patience and good humour, never giving up on the battle that had been waged, without the need for words, over their only child. For Ziggy, the battle had been no contest. She was her father's daughter and he had known it.

'Why don't you ask him for yourself?' The cool voice cut into her painful thoughts and she forced herself to meet the dark assessive eyes of the man who looked at her as though she were an insect on a pin.

'I've already told you,' she replied stonily, 'I don't want anything to do with him. He drove my father away, so he can't expect me to come running when he calls. So you can tell him that when you report back.'

'Aren't you even going to read his letter?' He spoke with a patience that had to be strained—it was too obviously schooled to be anything otherwise—and he got to his feet, standing over her, making her feel like a small threatened animal. And that was a totally new experience for her, so, more to get rid of him than anything else, she ripped open the envelopes.

The first was a copy of her father's birth certificate and she'd keep that, for sentiment's sake, but the second envelope held a sheet of thick, crested paper and a few imperiously scrawled words, and after scanning it, she crumpled it slowly in one white-knuckled hand, her tone scornfully dismissive as she told him, 'It reads like a rather impolite royal command. He desires me to accompany you on a visit to Staineswick—wherever that is—and that's it. No "Please" or "Would you" or anything remotely civil! And who the hell——' azure eyes narrowed suspiciously '—are you, anyway? His butler, or something?'

'No, not exactly.' The slight smile he gave her raised goose-bumps and she knew that he knew she wasn't going to like what he had to say, and he was right, because when he told her, matter-of-factly, 'Following your father's death, I'm Lord Staineswick's heir,' Ziggy felt sick with resentment. This urbane, arrogant, over-privileged swine was actually taking her father's place. It made her feel ill just to think about it! No wonder Dad had never mentioned his family background. For as long as she could remember he'd never had a good word to say for the over-privileged of this world, or for those who inherited vast amounts of wealth, having done nothing to earn it. And if this Rafe d'Anjou character was anything to go by then she wholeheartedly endorsed her father's opinions! But another, calmer thought occurred, and she voiced it cuttingly.

'You're welcome to what my father chose to leave behind him. He wasn't interested in outdated titles or inherited property, so, as I said, you're welcome to what pickings he was man enough to turn his back on.'

Rafe d'Anjou shrugged, his eyes narrowing dangerously, his voice a whiplash of derision,

'Since, as far as we know, your father never learned of his elder brother's death and his own position as Lord Staineswick's heir, your heated defence is debatable.'

Staring at him, Ziggy felt her cheeks burn with the insulting insinuation, and she opened her mouth to tell him to get out before she threw him out, but he held up a pacifying hand and stopped the words in her throat as he added, amazing her,

'I'm sorry, I shouldn't have said that. No one will ever know what your father's reaction would have been had he learned he was his father's heir. Now, won't you reconsider? Maybe the Earl's letter was terse, but I know your grandfather and I know he would have found it difficult to express, through the written word, his deep desire to heal the family rift.'

If Ziggy hadn't known better she would have sworn she could detect a note of pleading in that smooth, cultured voice. But his next words drove all such thoughts clear out of sight.

'I'll be leaving for Staineswick tomorrow morning. I'll pick you up here at ten. You don't need to bring anything other than a change of clothing—my mother will see that you have something more suitable to wear.' His eyes travelled over her with a look that was a whisper away from an insult, and Ziggy's face flamed. Beginning to walk away, he turned, his eyes deriding her. 'You won't need to come back to this place, so if you're in any difficulty over owed rent, or any other financial matter, I'll sort it all out in the morning.'

Wildly, Ziggy tried to grapple with the implications of what he had said, and the only thing that stood out clearly was that she was being taken over. She had no doubts that her grandfather was who this man said he was, she had seen the copy of the birth certificate and had read the Earl's letter of command. Besides, Rafe d'Anjou wouldn't be here talking to her at all, if it weren't absolutely necessary.

But he was already on his way to the door and so far she hadn't made him understand that she was serious about not obeying her grandfather's imperious command. And who in the world was this guy's mother, for pity's sake!

She scrambled to her feet and he turned to face her blandly as she growled, 'Just hang on a minute there, will you!' She was shaking again, and she didn't know why because, after all, he couldn't make her do anything she didn't want to do. And firmly into that category came driving to Staineswick—wherever that was—with him, or seeing her grandfather.

'Yes?' The impatience expressed by the slight narrowing of the deep grey eyes, the barely noticeable compression of the sensual male mouth, was subtle. There was nothing crude or obvious about this man and, because of that, his aura of superiority was all the more devastating, incensing her so that her long, slender hands balled into fists at her sides as she informed him frigidly,

'I'm not going anywhere, that's for starters. And this *place* is my home, and I share it with my friends and I work with my friends, and that's the way it's going to be until *I* decide otherwise. Understand?'

'Succinctly put,' he told her drily. 'But I hardly think the Earl would approve of the haphazard way you earn a living, or wish his granddaughter to live in such a place. However,' he shrugged minimally, 'that's beside the point. Your grandfather is most anxious to see you,' he stated again with superb patience, though his eyes told her that he for one couldn't understand why.

Turning back into the body of the room, he stationed himself with his back to the grate where an unsavoury mess of screwed up fish and chip wrappers, empty crisp bags and cigarette ends waited for someone, some time, to put a match to them.

Ziggy, staring at him with glittering eyes, hated him for the way he so easily made her surroundings seem suddenly unbearably squalid and herself little better. Breathing hard now, her delicately rounded breasts rising and falling rapidly beneath the shapeless T-shirt, she curled her upper lip, displaying sharp white teeth.

'Give me one good reason why I should do as his *lordship*,' she stressed insultingly, 'so anxiously wishes.'

She registered the flicker of anger that darkened his eyes and almost admired him for the way he controlled it as he answered evenly,

'Because he's an old man, a sick man. Because you're his closest blood kin. Because he would like to get to know you in the time he has left. And if those aren't reasons enough,' again the muted shaft of anger, 'you too are his heir. The unentailed Staineswick property will eventually belong to you. That, and a great deal of money.'

Ziggy flopped in the chair he had used earlier. Her legs had suddenly given way, and her brow puckered anxiously as she tried to come to terms with what he had told her.

She didn't want to inherit anything. She didn't want to see her grandfather. She wanted to be left alone to make her own life.

'How did you find me?' she asked dully. She wished he hadn't. All this talk of earls and property, of her father's aristocratic roots, had rekindled the depression that had clung so deeply and stubbornly after his death. Brought him so vividly back to mind. He had wanted no part of his elevated background, so neither did she.

'Easily. Tracing you back to London was relatively simple,' Rafe d'Anjou said tonelessly. 'Finding your father in the first instance was, apparently, more difficult. When his older son, Dudley, died twelve years ago, Lord Staineswick hired a firm of investigators to trace Edward, your father. After Dudley's death he became his father's heir. It took eighteen months to track him down to Vancouver, where it was learned he had a wife and daughter.'

'Dad never mentioned being contacted by his family,' Ziggy said huskily, disbelievingly, and Rafe d'Anjou informed her drily,

'As far as I know, he wasn't. Having had him traced, we must assume that Lord Staineswick was satisfied. It was enough to receive reports of his movements from time to time, so that he could be contacted immediately when the need arose.'

'But Dad died,' Ziggy said thickly, her eyes half closed as she retreated into prickly defensiveness, and Rafe's voice was almost gentle as he commented quietly,

'It was your father's wish to cut himself off from his family. He knew where to find them if he wanted them.'

The cool logic of that remark didn't help. All she could think of was the fact that the Earl had known—for over ten years—exactly where his estranged son was. And he hadn't troubled himself to even bother to write, to try to heal the wound that had been inflicted all those years ago. A wound that must have been deep enough, sharp enough, to make a young man of twenty leave home and family and never look back.

So no way was she going to pander to the old man's wishes now. She would be betraying her father if she did, betraying herself. And she wanted d'Anjou out.

The potent chemistry that had sparked antagonism to life between them was increasing with startling virility with every second that passed, and she wanted him out, out of here, out of her life, and ultimately, out of her mind.

But it would be a long time before she would rid herself of the sour taste this interview had left behind.

The ten minutes she had said he could have had stretched to over an hour, and she still had to trek to the launderette. Life, as they said, had to go on, even if her world had turned on its heels. But Rafe seemed able to pin her to her chair with those cold, clever eyes, to subjugate her by the power of his personality alone so that she couldn't find the words to tell him to leave and never come back...

And that cool, elegant voice was filling her mind, even though she had no wish to admit it.

'I know this must have come as a shock; nobody re-alised that your father neglected to tell you the facts of your ancestry. However, once you've had time to con-sider the implications of what you've learned, I'm sure you'll be able to adapt to your future.'

Desperately, Ziggy tried to close out his sardonic voice, to summon the willpower to tell him where to put the Earl and her inheritance—and her future, as he and her grandfather saw it. And she was pitifully grateful when the clatter of her friends' feet on the stairs, the sound of their voices, helped her to get a hold on herself.

Not listening to what he was saying now, she was on her feet as the door burst open, Kate and Sam first, their arms round each other, Damien bringing up the rear, his eyes narrowing as he looked from Ziggy to Rafe d'Anjou.

Sam dropped into an armchair, pulling Kate with him, and Damien, crossing to her side, put his arms round her.

'Everything OK, lover?'

She wasn't his lover, hadn't been any man's lover, come to that, and she disliked the hot moist feel of his hand as he slid it beneath the hem of the loose T-shirt, his fingers finding her cool naked skin. Disliked it but endured it, because at least Damien was on her side and she wanted to show d'Anjou that she had allies. His fingers moved upwards, over her ribs, and she could smell the beer on his breath and tried not to wrinkle her nose in disgust. But if he went any further, if she felt his hand on her breast, she would slap him! Never mind the warped satisfaction she was getting from seeing the barely disguised distaste on Rafe d'Anjou's face as his cold eyes followed the progress of Damien's hand. 'Peasants Petting'—she could almost read the title of the mind picture he would be receiving!

'I thought he'd have been long gone,' sneered Damien. 'Want me to ask him to leave?'

Maybe Damien resented the intrusion of such an obviously superior specimen on his patch, Ziggy didn't know, and she wasn't much interested in the psychology behind Damien's flare of belligerence, and however he 'asked' d'Anjou to leave, he would go when he was ready and not before.

But the situation had its amusing aspects, and she added her own neat barb. 'The heir apparent is just about to leave.'

Rafe d'Anjou dipped his head briefly, his slight smile denigrating, successfully placing her childish remark on the low plane it deserved, yet somehow promising retribution at a later date.

'Until tomorrow morning, Miss Bellingham. Ten o'clock,' and he was gone before she had time to restate that he'd have a wasted journey because at ten tomorrow she and her friends would be on their way to Covent Garden, about to embark on another day of 'unsuitable activity'.

Damien's fumblings were beginning to revolt her, and as soon as the door closed behind her unwelcome visitor she twisted away from him, reaching for the bag of washing she'd put ready earlier.

When she'd first arrived on the scene Damien had tried to get her into his bed, but she'd quickly put him straight on that score. She wasn't interested in casual sex, never had been, couldn't see the day dawning when she would be. He had accepted it with reasonable grace, but he was looking surly now, realising he'd been permitted liberties that wouldn't have been tolerated but for the presence of that alien well-heeled stranger. In a way he couldn't understand, he had been used, and he didn't like that. And Kate said, round-eyed, 'What was that about an heir apparent? What's going on around here?'

'A joke,' Ziggy dismissed tightly, not wanting to enlighten them because she wasn't feeling very enlightened herself. She grabbed the plastic carrier of laundry and let herself out. She'd dream up something to explain Rafe d'Anjou's visit. She certainly wasn't going to tell them about the Earl and all that stuff. There was no point. In a strange way, the news had embarrassed her, and she wouldn't be visiting her grandfather and she wouldn't be inheriting anything, either. Or if she did, eventually, she would refuse to accept it, whatever it was. She wanted nothing from Lord Staineswick. She was going to forget all about him, and Rafe d'Anjou, on that she was quite determined.

*   *   *

They had left the motorway several miles behind and the
Silver Spirit was heading into the Shropshire hills, but
Ziggy stared straight ahead, seeing nothing of the twisting
narrow lanes with their foaming verges of Queen Anne's
lace or the quiet, time-touched villages they passed
through. She was too edgily aware of Rafe at her side,
of his silence, to be able to absorb anything else.

He could be said to be concentrating on his driving,
but she knew there was more to his silence than that.
She could feel the thoughts that inhabited his head as if
they were her own. And they were far from flattering.

At ten that morning, with one unpleasant scene
already behind her, she had been at her most defensive
when the elegant Rolls had pulled up at the crumbling
kerb outside the tall dingy house in Bethnal Green.

'So you're walking out on us, just like that!' Damien
had accused, justly infuriated, Ziggy had to admit, by
her sudden decision to cut loose from the troupe.

'I'll be back,' she had promised, stuffing her be-
longings into her duffle bag, but he'd said, 'Don't count
on it, lover. If you walk out on us we'll find someone
else. That you *can* count on.'

She hadn't figured on staying with the troupe for very
much longer, but she had intended to give them good
warning. She hadn't wanted to leave them on a sour note,
but Rafe d'Anjou hadn't left her much choice.

Right up until four a.m. she had been quite sure that
she would have nothing whatsoever to do with the old
man who had cared so little for his lost and estranged
son that even when he had tracked him down he hadn't
bothered to write, to try to heal the breach that went
way back into the past. Her father had been a loving
man and would not have cut home and family out of
his life without good reason. She was fiercely partisan,

and whatever had caused the quarrel must have been her grandfather's fault, and he had been too uncaring to try to put it right. Her loyalties were deep, and they were staunchly with her father.

And the more she had lain awake, pondering the events of the day, the more she had wished her father were alive to give his advice. But if her father were alive, none of this would have happened. The Earl had only made his move after the death of the son he hadn't wanted to know.

It had been then, uncomfortably tossing and turning in the sleeping bag she used on the kitchen floor—the only space available unless she wanted to use the sofa in the living area where Damien slept on a folding bed arrangement, which she definitely didn't—that the idea of confronting her grandfather insinuated itself into her head. Far from answering his imperious summons in a spirit of reconciliation, a willingness to—how had the d'Anjou character put it?—to adapt to her future as a considerable heiress, she would tell him that he need not look to her to inherit his wealth and part of his property, to be a dutiful granddaughter. She stood where her father had chosen to stand, outside the influence of the Earls of Staineswick. She would also throw in a few words on the intransigence of a man who was devious enough to put private investigators on the trail of his, by then, only son, but had been too mean-minded to come out into the open, to declare himself and try to build bridges over the long years of cold silence.

This decided, Ziggy had slept for three hours, waking at seven when Kate padded into the kitchen, yawning, running her fingers through her short brown hair, putting the kettle on for tea.

And when the Rolls had arrived Ziggy had been ready, dressed in faded jeans and a scarlet T-shirt, her bare feet stuffed into thonged sandals, her glossy hair braided into two forward-falling plaits.

Rafe's frostily civil greeting had told her as clearly as if he had voiced his thoughts aloud what he thought of her appearance, of the scruffy duffle bag which contained her worldly possessions—the sleeping bag rolled up and tied on with an old leather belt.

Disposing of the obviously despised luggage in the boot, he had opened the passenger door for her and she'd sunk into the luxury of the superbly comfortable leather upholstery, struck yet again by the sheer daunting presence of the man, the style, the indefinable something that went far deeper than his undeniably fascinating good looks, his air of impeccable breeding, of inborn superiority.

He put her immediately on the defensive, caused hackles she hadn't known she had to bristle.

She glanced across at him as he settled behind the wheel, her heart rattling angrily against her ribs as she registered the insolence of the slight smile he gave her, the passionate curve of his full lower lip more than hinting at powerful emotions that would be all the more devastating for the strength of will shown in the depths of the cold grey eyes, the hard masculine moulding of brow and jaw and starkly jutting cheekbones.

The car sprang to potent purring life beneath his hands and as they pulled away Ziggy thought, I pity his wife. The stray thought took root, fed by his arrogant silence, and her mind wandered amusedly, elaborating on the plight of the unknown woman.

She would be mousy and timid and frightfully proper—the drab peahen, not presuming to vie with the

sartorial or physical splendour of her superior mate. She
would dress and behave exactly as he decreed. Twinsets
and pearls and baggy but well-pedigreed tweeds, she
supposed. She would probably ride to hounds and certainly be very good at gardening. She would head various
committees, wearing suitable hats, and give nice little
dinner parties wearing ill-fitting satin and lots of drapes
because, from what Ziggy had heard, the owners of
English country houses hadn't yet got around to in-
stalling central heating and had to wear thermal underwear beneath everything between October and June. And
she would visit the peasants in their broken little estate
cottages, bearing gifts of unwanted kitchen scraps...

At this point, recognising the absurdity of her
thoughts, Ziggy broke into irrepressible giggles, and
Rafe, waiting for the traffic lights to change, said, 'Share
the joke?'

'I was just trying to picture your wife,' Ziggy stated,
realising, too late, how rude that must sound—coupled
with her obvious amusement. And his mouth curled as
if he'd read her thoughts.

'I don't have one, so don't waste your time. The idea
of tying myself down to that extent hasn't appealed so
far.'

Which made sense, whichever way you looked at it,
Ziggy decided, watching a couple of pedestrians scurry
across in front of them before the lights changed. On
the one hand there probably wasn't a woman alive who'd
be fool enough to place herself under this man's domi-
nation. Nowadays, most men believed that a wife was
a partner, not a chattel, but not this man. Male arrogance positively oozed from every pore; he was a
throwback. But, on the other hand, he was probably

incapable of committing himself to any one woman for
life—even if one could be found who was stupid enough
to take him on. He looked the type who would be choosy
about female companionship of the more intimate kind—
very choosy—but not to the extent of ever loving one
of that select number more than he loved himself. He
was the up-market version of the love 'em and leave 'em
type!

Then a rather distasteful thought occurred, and she
voiced it with the air of one resigned to cope with unpleasant truths now and then.

'If you're my grandfather's heir, then I guess that
makes us cousins, or something.'

'Not quite.' His sideways glance was almost amused,
or maybe that slight quirking of the hard male mouth
denoted relief? 'After your father's death I became your
grandfather's heir as the closest surviving relative of the
direct male line. In fact, my branch of the Bellingham
family springs from your grandfather's uncle. Any relationship between you and me is very distant.'

'That's the best news I've had all week.' Ziggy softened
the rudeness with a wide grin, then added suspiciously,
'So why isn't your name Bellingham? What's with the
fancy foreign-sounding handle?'

He took his eyes off the road for long enough to give
her a withering look. 'My father married a French girl,
Léonie d'Anjou, and as part of the marriage contract
he agreed to take her name. That, again, had something
to do with family property. Anything else you want to
know?'

As he clearly thought her a pest of the first water Ziggy
decided to needle him some more. It was fun, in a way,
and probably the only weapon she had against his aura

of superior male dominance, so she injected a note of pique in her voice.

'So a mere female, even if she is a direct descendant, has to make way for some remote half-foreigner who doesn't even bear the family name simply because he happens to be a male. Talk about the equality of the sexes!'

Ziggy had no wish to inherit anything, not even the proverbial silver spoon her father had been born with—the silver spoon he had obviously tossed aside as being worthless! But the d'Anjou monster wasn't to know that, and he replied sarcastically, 'Don't get too upset about it, child. The unentailed part of your grandfather's property, which includes a healthy amount of hard cash, should be adequate, even for you.'

Which made her sound greedy, out for all she could get, and that was far from being the case. But she wasn't about to put him straight, because he could think what he liked. His opinion of her wasn't worth a moment's discomfort. However, something else was bothering her now and she said quickly,

'The way you talk, it sounds like the Earl is gasping his last,' and that was bad news, because it meant this journey was wasted. No matter how badly the old man had treated her beloved father, there was no way she could give a dying man a large and sour slice of her mind.

But he answered with infuriating dryness, 'Sorry to disappoint you, but you'll have to wait for your hand-out for a while yet—I hope. Your grandfather's good for a few more years, if he takes care. He had a heart attack a week after he heard of your father's death—and that scared us badly. My mother's been at Staineswick since then, making sure he does take care of himself, and of course, I spend as much time there as I can.'

I'll just bet you do! Ziggy thought vehemently, deeply resenting the way he'd taken her query about her grandfather's health to mean she had hopes of getting her hands on as much as she could as soon as she could. She had no doubt at all that the vile Rafe d'Anjou had come scurrying along the moment he heard that the old man he was heir to was ill. So if he thought she was a vulture, what did that make him? And the only reason she was in this car, with this beast, was to give her grandfather a slice of her mind. But she wouldn't demean herself by explaining that. No, sir. He would discover the true reason for her visit soon enough.

At last, stiff with holding herself in smouldering loathing of the man at her side, Ziggy exhaled a long sigh of relief as he turned the Silver Spirit between tall stone pillars set in a seemingly endless high stone wall. Journey's end, at long last.

Ornate wrought-iron gates, bearing the family crest, stood open, giving access to a paved drive which ran for miles through parkland where sheep grazed beneath stands of oak and beech, over cattle grids and on through an avenue of newly budding limes.

At the crest of a rise he surprised her by halting the car, cutting the engine, and the silence was intense. She could have sworn she could actually hear the sudden acceleration of her heartbeats as her eyes were drawn to the great house, still half a mile distant.

It was formidable, yet achingly beautiful; a magnificent piece of Tudor architecture created in mellow stone, sunlight glinting back from the tall mullioned windows in the two symmetrical out-thrusting bays on either side of the great main door.

The electrically operated window at Rafe's side slid silently down, admitting the breath of air, cool and fresh with the scent of newly growing things, and Ziggy, unable to pull her awed and fascinated eyes from the first sighting of the place that had been her father's home, his unknown inheritance for about twelve years, heard the battened-down distaste in the cold dark voice as Rafe angled himself back against the door, facing her.

'A word to the wise—and I'd stake my life you're that, at least where wisdom touches your financial expectations.'

She turned to face him reluctantly, her shoulders stiffening, her azure eyes wary as she waited for yet more of his insults. She was half inclined to get out and walk the remaining distance, but was held by his sheer hypnotic presence. She was repelled by, and yet drawn to, a mysterious something in him that all her instincts translated as danger.

'As you plainly regarded Lord Staineswick's invitation as a cast-iron ticket to a great inheritance I want you to think carefully about the way you react to him. I don't want you to appear too crass, too greedy. Not for your sake, I hasten to say, but for his. I'm fond of him. I don't want to see him hurt.'

His voice had a quiet, punitive quality that lashed her and his dislike was distilled to pure venom in the close confines of the car. Ziggy might have cringed under the weight of it, but she had an abundance of challenging pride in her own right, and boy, was she glad of that now!

So she lifted her delicate, pointed chin and snapped, 'Save your lectures for someone who'll listen, because I'm damned sure I won't!'

She was already groping for the door lock, ready to get out and walk, but his fingers fastened around her arm, jerking her back, his eyes smouldering with an anger she knew would be catastrophic if it were ever to be fully ignited.

'You will listen, if it's the last thing you do on this earth, Miss Bellingham. And you will listen well,' he dismissed contemptuously, abruptly releasing her trapped arm, holding her with his eyes, his disgust. 'I promised I'd bring you to your grandfather, and I keep my word. So I went to Canada, to your last address, traced your mother to Calgary and learned you were visiting London. It took longer, there, to find you because you were no longer at the address your mother gave me. And when I did find you I almost wished I hadn't. Not because of the way you were trying to earn a living,' he dismissed impatiently, 'but for the way you are. You're bad news, Ziggy Bellingham, last of the direct line. Bad news for your grandfather, bad news for Staineswick. A sharp-tongued, greedy virago with the morals of an alley cat. I don't say this lightly,' he injected as she opened her mouth on a howl of protest. 'I formed my opinions, soundly, I think, on the basis of the way you greeted my simple request for a few minutes of your time—time which I had already paid for, by the way—of the way you live, the man you live with, your immediate change of attitude when you learned that your grandfather was not merely an old man who wanted to get to know his grandchild at last, but a peer of the realm, disposed to leave a great deal of property in your hands because you're his only close blood kin.'

Ziggy scowled at him, her face burning with scalding colour as she rubbed her arm, where his fingers had bitten savagely into soft flesh, trying to disperse the strangely electrifying sensation that obstinately remained.

She had known his opinion of her was rock-bottom, but she hadn't cared, certainly not enough to put him right. And now he was calmly spelling it out, holding nothing back, and she would have given much to have what it took to slap the derisive curl from his mouth as he went on acidly, 'I don't want to see you displaying your greed or your ignorance. You've asked nothing about your grandfather—except about his possible demise!'

That remark stung, but she guessed she'd asked for it, and she contented herself with an icy glare as he went on cuttingly, 'What do you know of your father's family?'

'Not much,' she shrugged dismissively, feeling slightly easier because he had shifted his position, not facing her now, his hands touching the steering wheel lightly, and she told him frigidly, 'Dad never spoke about his parents, or his brother, come to that. All I knew about his earlier life in England—and that wasn't much—came from my mother. And the details were pretty scant, things she'd picked up from Dad, or guessed, and I never took much notice because if Dad had wanted to leave it all behind, then I didn't want to know either. Satisfied?' she snapped. 'If so, let's get going, I've had as much of your company as is good for my temper.'

Rafe did look at her then, the cool dark grey eyes taking in the flush of pride, the mutinous lift of the pointed chin, and he commented with aggravating con-descension, 'You've certainly inherited your father's stubborness,' then clipped on, 'I'll fill you in, since you can't be bothered to ask—your grandmother died when your father was fifteen, and five years later he took off and wasn't heard of until the Earl instigated a search for him following the death of his elder son, Dudley. Dudley died unmarried, so that meant your father, had he lived, would have inherited the title and entail.'

But her father hadn't known of his brother's death, Ziggy was sure of that. Would he have returned to Staineswick, to claim his inheritance, had he known? She thought not. And yet she was here, staring at the house where he had been born, and tears threatened. To stem them, to stop herself from dwelling on the shock and pain of his death, she said stingingly, 'So Grandfather rushed around and winkled you out of the woodwork, did he? Not a direct descendant, but you'd have to do. And once you'd got over celebrating your good fortune you rushed over here, bringing your mother along, anxious to get your feet under the baronial table and enjoy the life of privilege that had gratifyingly dropped into your life like a big fat plum! Did you give up your job? Hang around here for whatever you could wheedle out of the old man? And how do you pass your time now you're a man with prospects? Driving expensive cars? Choosing new and expensive suits? Telling my grandfather just how *fond* of him you are?'

Silently, one dark brow speakingly raised, Rafe started the car, letting it idle over the crest down towards the waiting house. And Ziggy, bristling now because she thought she was beginning to see just why he had treated her with patronising distaste all along the line, growled, 'No wonder you've been looking down your elegant nose at me! It has nothing to do with the way I lived, or who I lived with, and why, has it? You wish you'd never found me because I'm a threat, aren't I?' She folded her arms, smiling grimly because she knew she'd found the answer. 'Without me, Grandfather would leave everything to you, wouldn't he? You said yourself that a healthy amount of cash was involved, and you'd rather it wasn't hived off, wouldn't you? Tough!'

He didn't answer that piece of nastiness; she hadn't expected him to. But she hoped her perspicacity would give him something to think about, plus a few sleepless nights, because never, ever had she met anyone who got under her skin the way he did. And if the odious object had visions of her ingratiating herself with her long-lost grandfather, and dropping poisoned darts about 'how *awful* Rafe had been to her'—because entails could be broken, couldn't they, and the heir could find himself with nothing more than a worthless title?—then his sleepless nights could be peopled with waking nightmares!

Not that she had any intention of trying to do any such thing. She wouldn't even hang around for her own inheritance—let alone try to take his. Because whatever her future fortune, good or bad, it would be of her own making. The Earl could leave every stick and stone, and every last penny, to Rafe d'Anjou as far as she was concerned. But he wasn't to know that, was he? And she didn't care how badly he thought of her, did she?

CHAPTER THREE

'I HAVE to talk to you, Grandfather.' Ziggy put her empty coffee cup aside and mentally squared up to what had to be said, trying to order her thoughts, assemble the accusing words without actually damaging his health! But the process was halted as Dudley, tenth Earl of Staineswick, her grandfather, surprised her yet again as he concurred readily,

'Yes. We have a great deal to say, and it won't be easy for either of us. But there's good will on my part, and, I hope, on yours?'

Ziggy wasn't too sure about that. Sitting on the library floor at her grandfather's feet, she still felt in a state bordering on shock. She had been in it since Rafe had handed her over to the housekeeper, Mrs Thurston, almost twenty-four hours ago. Thurston, the butler, had met them at the head of the broad stone steps yesterday afternoon, his politely impassive features giving nothing away, not even curiosity, but Mrs Thurston had said, 'Welcome home, Miss Ziggy,' as if she were a valued member of the family.

And meeting her grandfather for the first time an hour later had disturbed her far more than she had expected or liked, had driven some of the belligerent defensiveness that had ridden her out of her mind.

The frail, elderly man who had risen from a winged armchair in this very room had seemed uncannily familiar to her. He had reminded her so strongly of her father that other thoughts had, for the time being, left her head.

It was the look in his hazel eyes, the way he carried his head, the way he smiled. It had been like looking at a time-projection, and Ziggy's eyes had been as misty as the old man's as she had unthinkingly gone to the outstretched arms he had held to her.

Behind her, she had heard Rafe's soft grunt of derision, had almost heard the slow handclap he would have produced had the Earl been deaf and blind. She had almost forgotten his presence in the shock of seeing the man who looked exactly like her father might have done had he lived another twenty-five years.

Rafe's expression had been as cold as permafrost when he'd collected her from the room Mrs Thurston had given her, and after the terse injunction that she was summoned to meet Lord Staineswick, he had led the way through the bewilderingly large and lovely house without uttering another word.

Ziggy's resentment had still been riding high at that time, against her grandfather and Rafe, her intention to say her piece and get the hell out of here at first light in the morning still filling her mind. That was until she had actually come face to face with her grandfather, felt the frail old arms close around her, heard the raw emotion in the old voice as he'd said, 'Thank you for coming. You can't know how much I need to have you here, how long I've waited for you.'

So she couldn't, as she'd originally intended, hurl bitter recriminations at the old man and then walk out. Nothing seemed so clear-cut or simple any more, and before she began to speak her mind she knew she had to discover what had caused the rift between her father and grandfather, and find out exactly why the Earl hadn't attempted to contact his surviving son once he had discovered his whereabouts.

Today had dawned chilly with a mizzle of rain, and after a solitary breakfast the summons to have coffee with her grandfather in the library had almost been welcome. Sitting cross-legged on the fine Aubusson carpet, Ziggy stared reflectively into the flames which leapt in the deep stone hearth. Barefoot, wearing shabby jeans and a shrunken grey wool sweater, her heavy hair formed into a single thick braid, she knew she looked like an urchin, out of place in the sumptuous room where all the walls, save the huge velvet-curtained window alcove, were lined with bookcases. She was her normal casual self, out of place, and knew she could never fit into this exquisite, privileged background in a million years, and had no intention of trying.

She had been bemused into an unacceptable state of quiescence by the sheer size and magnificence of her father's birthplace, by the Earl's resemblance to the father she had idolised, by the unaccountable joy he had shown on her arrival. And his gentle talk, of days gone by, of the present need to turn a profit, the predictable opening of the great house to the public, had held her enthralled attention so far.

But it was time to turn her attention to the real purpose behind her visit. To go on her way, a way which would never again bring her into the exalted orbit of the Earl of Staineswick. This morning's brief respite was nothing more than a vaguely surrealistic dream; the reality of her life, her future, was something else again. She had to find out what she needed to know, then leave.

'Grandfather——' her normal forthrightness seemed, incomprehensibly, to have deserted her, and as she met his unwavering eyes she had to force a tinge of asperity to her words. 'I need to know why you quarrelled with

Dad. What could have been so terrible that it kept father and son apart for thirty years?'

'What could have been so terrible?' he echoed slowly, the words hoarse. 'An old man's stubbornness and a young man's pride. Terrible things indeed.'

Ziggy's eyes searched his features, bleak and drawn now, and for the first time she felt the unwilling stirrings of real compassion. Whatever had happened all those years ago obviously still had the power to hurt, and she said rapidly, and didn't know where the words had come from, because upsetting him, striking a blow for her father, had been the reason for her presence here, 'I don't want to upset you.'

'It has to be said.' He met her eyes steadily and she was unwillingly touched by the love she saw there. 'You have every right to question me, and every right to a truthful answer. As you know, I had two sons. Dudley, my heir, and Edward, your father.' He leaned heavily back in his chair, and Ziggy tried not to worry over how tired he suddenly looked.

'Of the two,' he went on slowly, 'Edward was by far the stronger character, the one who cared about Staineswick. It meant nothing to Dudley, I'm afraid, except as a bottomless money-pot. Even when they were boys I knew your father would have made the better heir. He knew it too, and it rankled. Your father knew that if Dudley inherited he would allow the house and land to rot. It meant nothing to him, so long as there were paintings and furniture to sell—and the unentailed land—to finance his hedonistic lifestyle. Your grandmother and I tried everything we knew to get him to face up to his responsibilities, but nothing got through, and after she died things got worse. And about four years later, after some particularly spectacular piece of stupidity on Dudley's part, your father begged me to break the entail and make him my heir. Dudley could have the title—it was worthless—but Edward wanted control of the property. It could have been done,' he sighed heavily, and Ziggy had to remind herself that she had no reason to feel pity for the man who had coldly ignored his son and his family for all those years. 'Yes, it could have been done, but I was stubborn. And the more your father told me where my duty lay, the more intractable I became—I see that now. All I could point out was that Dudley was the firstborn, my heir, and that it was Edward's duty to try to be a moderating influence on his brother.'

'So Dad left?' Ziggy said quietly, and the Earl nodded.

'The next day. He told me he wouldn't take second place to any man, and certainly not to one so totally inept and decadent. He told me he was washing his hands of the lot of us, of outworn traditions and what he termed effete, aristocratic pigheadedness. He never came back.'

The sad silence of impotent regret cast its pall over the room, and Ziggy shivered, remembering the fierce independence, that sometimes-felt sense of a deep and nameless anger that had been a facet of the personality of the father she had adored. She understood it now.

'But you didn't tell him when Dudley died; you had him traced, but you didn't try to heal the breach,' she pointed out tersely. What was past was past, and nothing could be altered by inflicting more hurt on the old man who was now hurting enough, but she knew she had to make this one last stand, for her father's sake. But she was shaken by his rapid reply.

'But I did!' He shot her a pleading look beneath shaggy white brows. 'For years I'd expected Edward to come home, and the fact that he didn't grieved me deeply.' His mouth curved in a mocking half-smile. 'He'd gone of his own free will, and for years I'd lived in a fool's paradise, telling myself that he'd come back one day, his tail between his legs. Staineswick was in his blood, I assured myself, he wouldn't be able to stay away. But he did, and my own error of judgement piqued me, I suppose. But when Dudley was killed, driving one of those fast cars he was too damned fond of, it became imperative that Edward was contacted. Eventually he was. He was living in Canada with his wife and child. And that hurt. I had a grandchild, and he hadn't told me, didn't ever intend telling me, as far as I knew. I thought I'd never be able to forgive him for that. But I flew out—without anyone back here knowing what I was up to—and sent the investigator I'd hired up to the Fraser River area where your father was working at the time. I sent a letter, telling him of Dudley's death and asking him to see me. He eventually came to my hotel in Vancouver. It was a painful meeting for both of us. I asked him to return to Staineswick, to bring his family, to take his place as my heir.'

'And he refused?' Ziggy questioned huskily, unwillingly conceding that she couldn't have known her father as well as she thought she had. That he had kept that kind of secret from her and her mother seemed unbelievable. And it hurt. It made her feel she had never known him, that in an odd way he hadn't trusted her enough to tell her the truth of his origins. Yet she couldn't doubt the veracity of what her grandfather had just told her. 'He didn't tell us you'd been to see him,' she muttered hoarsely.

'My dear.' He put a gentle hand over hers, sympathy and understanding in the kind old eyes. 'You mustn't

let that trouble you. Your father loved you deeply, more
than anything in the world—he told me that. And after
all, at the time you were about eleven years old and I
don't suppose he felt it would serve any useful purpose
to tell you about my visit. As he said himself, you were
all ordinary Canadian citizens, and proud of it, with no
pretensions to anything, certainly not to the decadent
pull of the outdated tenets of a worn-out aristocracy. He
provided for his family by his own efforts, and his future
was in Canada—without the so-called benefits of inherited wealth and privilege. Neither of us came out of
that encounter well, I'm afraid. He allowed his pride to
blind him, and I was stubborn.' He shrugged heavily,
and Ziggy, feeling the weight of those long years of
silence, could have wept as he continued, 'And so I came
back here and was kept informed of my son's movements. And so I learned of his death, and sent Rafe for
you. I don't intend to lose you too, Ziggy.'

Tears filled her eyes, but there was nothing she could
say to that. She needed time to think over the implications of what she had learned before she could commit
herself to staying here, getting to know her grandfather
better, and if he was waiting for a reply to his unspoken
question she couldn't give one. Not now, perhaps not
ever...

'Ah, Rafe——' the sudden warmth in the Earl's voice,
the sound of the door opening, brought Ziggy's eyes
from their brooding contemplation of the burning fire
on the immense firedogs to the man who now stood in
the doorway.

He was wearing hip-hugging beige-coloured cords, a
dark green cashmere sweater, and she guessed drily that
he knew he presented a commanding figure. He had the
face and body of a conqueror—even if he was, in fact,

nothing more exalted than a hanger-on, an ageing earl's heir.

'Timed it just right, my boy! Ziggy's seen very little of the house—have you time to show her some of it before lunch? I'm afraid I'm no longer up to trekking around,' Lord Staineswick apologised wryly, laying an affectionate hand on Ziggy's smooth dark head. 'And I'd particularly like her to see her grandmother's portrait, then she'll understand why I said I'd been waiting for her for a great many years.'

Ziggy straightened her endless legs and got to her feet, stretching her supple body like a cat, not looking at Rafe but noting the twinkle of amusement in her grandfather's eyes. It stemmed from the inordinate amount of bare midriff which her unthinking stretching movement, combined with the shrunken grey sweater, had produced, she guessed. But at least he accepted her the way she was, took her unsuitable ragamuffin appearance in his stride.

'I'll wander round on my own. I'd prefer it, and I'm sure Rafe can find something more constructive to do with his time.' She didn't want to spend more time than was necessary with that sardonic, knowing man. Time spent in his undiluted presence would make her ill! But,

'There can be nothing more constructive than a properly conducted tour of the past that helped produce you,' the Earl said, straight-faced. 'And who better than Rafe, since I'm not up to it and Léonie won't be home before teatime.' He chuckled as he saw the flash of anger deep in Ziggy's eyes, but he dismissed them both smoothly enough, still master here despite his years and frailty. 'I'll expect an account of your reactions, my dear, at dinner this evening. Léonie will be with us, so we shall be quite a family party.'

Last night she had eaten from a tray in her room, but this evening, obviously, was going to be a formal occasion. She didn't want that. The longer she was here, the more she began to sympathise with, and understand, her grandfather, the more difficult it could become to make the old man understand that she had no intention of staying, or of coming back once she had gone.

'We'll do the gallery first, introduce you to your ancestors. That will give you a good crash-course into your family history.' Rafe smiled thinly, motioning her forward. But Ziggy stood her ground, leaning back against the library door which she had just closed behind her, staring mutinously into that devilishly self-assured face.

'I can see all I want to see on my own. And I'm not interested in history.'

'Not even your own family's?' A dark brow arched drily and she shrugged, the rise of her shoulders unconsciously elegant.

'The only family I've ever known—or what's left of it—is back home in Canada. Let's leave it at that.' She would have walked away, but a swift, graceful movement of his body stopped her, his sudden nearness having the effect of a current of electricity charging through her veins. It unnerved her, and her eyes were brilliant with something approaching fright as they clashed with his.

'Ziggy——' his tone was dangerously even '—your grandfather asked me to show you the portrait of your grandmother. We'll skip the rest for today, if you prefer.'

'And you always do as he asks!' Ziggy countered crossly, and he rocked back on his heels slightly, his hands pushed negligently into the pockets of the well-cut cords that clipped neat hips and long, long legs.

'I don't know why, Ziggy,' he began evenly, a trace of a smile tugging at one corner of his hard male mouth, 'but you appear to have a monumental chip on your shoulder. There really isn't any need for it, you're here now, accepted, and you and I have to make the best of it. So can't we at least try to be friends?'

He was making an effort, she thought derisively. Yesterday he had treated her like poison. Only that had been before he'd realised that the Earl was not about to tip the definitely unaristocratic last of the line out on her neck. And the offer of friendship just wasn't in character, because as far as he was concerned her grandfather's acceptance of her meant that a large amount of ready cash would one day leave the new heir's control. So maybe this new conciliatory approach was his sneaky way of ensuring that she didn't go to the Earl with tales of his arrogantly diabolical treatment of her!

But the drawly, slightly amused voice had brought her out in goose-bumps, and his nearness threatened her as nothing else ever had, and she didn't know why. But he surely wasn't going to get to know about that! So,

'I'd as soon make friends with a rattlesnake,' she told him, then, with a cool rudeness that almost took her own breath away, noting the dangerous narrowing of his eyes with a shiver of pure fear which she managed to hide behind a laid-back drawl, she said, 'Show me the painting, then you can crawl back to the Earl for a nice little pat on the head.'

She thought he was going to shake her for that insulting insinuation, and, to be honest, she wouldn't have blamed him. But nothing of her inner apprehension was allowed to show in the black-fringed eyes she coldly impaled him with. Though the azure depths did darken with relief as he merely swung away. That had been a

close-run thing! As it was, his controlled anger showed
only in the tautly moulded muscles of the wide angular
shoulders as he strode across the fine silken rugs that
were strewn on the floor of the vast hall and took the
gracefully soaring flight of stairs with their intricately
carved balustrading two at a time.

The wide, portrait-lined gallery at the head of the stairs
branched left and right, and as she resignedly drew level
with him he took her arm and turned to the right.

The muscles of his body were hard as steel beneath
the soft covering of cashmere, and Ziggy shuddered at
his touch, her bare feet stumbling as she tried to pull
away. But his grip only tightened and he glanced down
at her with mocking grey eyes, his mouth hardly moving
as he warned,

'Don't make too great an enemy of me.'

If that was a threat, it didn't impress her, and her chin
snapped up. 'You don't scare me!'

'No?' He slammed to a halt and she cannoned into
him and, more shocked by the close contact than she
dared to admit, even to herself, she danced away, as if
from the edge of an abyss, wrenching her arm free as
he lashed,

'Your volte-face regarding your grandfather and what
he can offer hasn't escaped me. Be careful that I don't
take it on myself to warn him of the true nature of his
loving grandchild! Or to tell him that she absolutely refused to have anything to do with him until I let it drop
that she stood to inherit enough to keep her in idle luxury
for the rest of her days!' His mouth curved witheringly,
and Ziggy's toes curled into the soft pile of the crimson
carpet as she contained the instinct to hit that handsome,
supercilious face.

But she wasn't going to give him the satisfaction of knowing how easily he could touch raw nerve-ends, and she snapped right back, 'Two can play that game! You haven't exactly welcomed me with open arms—and we both know why—so why don't I warn Grandfather about you! Blood is thicker than water, after all!' She fastened cool azure eyes on his face and growled, 'In fact, I'm surprised you haven't laid the poison already. You'd like nothing better than to see me thrown out on my ear—leaving you neatly in line for everything Grandfather has to leave.' She hated the way the talk of the inheritance was tossed around, as if the old man were already on his deathbed, and she hated Rafe's light shrug, the cold elegance of his voice as he dismissed her and her unmeant threats.

'Nothing's as simple as that, Ziggy. I wish to heaven it were.'

What he meant by that she didn't know, and it was with a sense of relief that she watched him walk briefly ahead, pausing in front of one of the gilt-framed portraits and reaching up to flick on the small shaded light tube that was necessary to provide the illumination for detailed scrutiny.

So this was Grandma, was it? Ziggy padded silently over and stood, hands on hips, slightly straddle-legged, to do her duty. A brief glance, a 'How nice', and she could make some excuse to wriggle away from his daunting presence.

Her mouth was already open to make some innocuous comment, and it stayed that way, her voice dying in her throat. The family resemblance between her father and her grandfather had been strong, but this was like looking into a mirror, except that the painted form of the young woman who looked endlessly out of the ornate frame

was obviously an aristocrat from the top of her artfully
piled raven-dark hair to the tips of the bejewelled fingers
which were loosely crossed in front of her, their whiteness
and purity of line elegant against the sumptuous sheen
of dull burgundy satin.

Sometimes her mother had teased her about her looks,
called her a changeling. Her father had never commented, though, on the fact that hazel-eyed, blond
parents had produced such an offspring. And sometimes, looking into the mirror when she'd been very much
younger, Ziggy had wondered where the slanting blue
eyes, the dark hair that almost glittered, and the creamy
white complexion had come from. Now she knew.

And she knew why her grandfather had accepted her
so immediately, why he had said he had been waiting
for her...

She turned aside, out of the illuminating glare of the
little light. She didn't want Rafe to see the glitter of tears
that stung her eyes, to know she could be so affected by
anything in this house. He said, 'Seen enough?' ex-
tinguishing the light. 'We'll have lunch now, Cook prepared it earlier.'

'You go ahead.' There was a gruffness in her voice
that he could interpret any way he chose. The portraits
of past Bellinghams stretched distantly along the gallery
walls in a blur of gilded frames and dim oil colours, but
the slanting painted azure eyes seemed almost to smile,
and Ziggy blinked furiously, sniffing, determinedly
talking her way out of the unwanted and dangerous sentimental state. 'I'm sure you'd prefer me to eat in the
servants' quarters. My table manners might be gruesome,
for all you know. And I wouldn't want to offend your
delicate sensibilities.'

She swung into her loose striding walk, her hands bunched into the pockets of her jeans, but Rafe caught up with her, falling in step.

'Don't be such a child! Cook has put a buffet lunch ready for the two of us, and I hope you're not going to be impossibly rude and ask for a tray in your room again.'

They had reached the head of the stairs, and although she'd intended to march straight ahead to the small sanctuary her room offered he caught her arm, angling her round. The look in his eyes made her feel like a stupid child, and she didn't normally sulk, but she felt dangerously near to that juvenile state now. So she snapped herself out of it and muttered 'OK' around the obstinate lump in her throat, following Rafe as he started down the stairs. After all, she couldn't expect to win all the time, she consoled herself. But her brow puckered thoughtfully as they descended the impressive staircase: she hadn't really won any of the rounds, had she? However much she had dug her heels in, protested, she had somehow always ended up doing precisely as he'd meant her to!

A fire was burning in the deeply recessed hearth of the small room Rafe called his study. He used it as an office, he said, and there were box files on the shelves that lined the walls—some leather-bound with cracked gold leaf dates, obviously old, some modern. There was a massive cluttered desk near the window and a gate-legged table was spread with a crisp snowy cloth and covered bowls which contained various salads, platters of cold pheasant and salmon, dishes of fresh fruit and a mouthwatering pavlova.

'You might prefer to tag on to one of the guided tours of the house this weekend,' suggested Rafe, pouring wine. 'The house itself is only open to the public on Saturdays and Sundays, and at least Hester won't make your hackles rise and she knows the family history backwards.'

Ziggy, buttering a crisp brown roll, didn't reply, and Rafe sat back in his seat, regarding her—the way she'd piled her plate like the half-starved waif she resembled— and Ziggy, glancing up, saw how the sensual male mouth indented with a fleeting shadow of secret amusement and thought no more of it, reapplying herself to the goodies on her plate.

He could smile his secret smile, she didn't give a damn, because the tempting display of food had made her realise how hungry she was. But as he began his own meal she paused, the loaded fork suspended halfway to her mouth, and tipped a delicately winged eyebrow in his direction.

'Hester? Who's Hester?'

'She does the tours of the house—she's the daughter of a neighbour, a Colonel Povey. As I said,' Rafe deftly squeezed a wedge of lemon over the portion of salmon on his plate, 'she knows everything there is to know of your family's history, and you might just listen to her, learn something.'

Attentively, he replenished her wineglass and Ziggy watched the foaming golden liquid in the crystal as he poured. She supposed she deserved that taunt, she had been impossibly rude to him all along the line. But then he had this terrible power to bring out the worst in her. He put her on edge, on the defensive, and her consequent rudeness was something he was going to have to learn to live with.

'Maybe I might, at that.' She helped herself to more salmon. It really was delicious. 'Grandfather was telling me about the Butterfly House—it sounded neat—it actually covers the costs?'

'And makes a profit,' Rafe told her with a sardonic twist to his mouth. 'This place doesn't run on pebbles and could easily become an historic millstone. But to attract sufficient tourists we need to offer more than a beautiful building to walk around. The Butterfly House does that. I'll take you over there in the morning, introduce you to Mike Wilson who runs the place, and you can look around before it opens to the paying public at ten.'

'I guess I can find my own way, and pay my entrance ticket.' Ziggy had a streak of independence a mile wide and she didn't want favours, not from him. But she didn't go as far as to say that, she had no intention of spoiling an excellent lunch by having yet another row with him.

'I dare say you can.' The tone was frigid now. 'Let's just say I'd like us to present a united front for your grandfather's sake. Pavlova?'

And guess why? Ziggy snorted to herself. To spike my guns if I decide to go wingeing to Gramps about the foul Rafe d'Anjou!

He ignored her mutinous glare, slicing into the delicious meringue and fruit concoction. 'And I would appreciate it if you could at least try to be polite to my mother when you meet her at dinner this evening. She's been visiting friends, but when I spoke to her on the phone last night she said she's longing to meet you— full of plans to take you shopping for clothes.'

'So I take it you told her how unsuitably I dressed,' fumed Ziggy, but Rafe ignored that; perhaps it was self-evident and needed no answer. He slid a slice of the pudding on to a delicate china plate and handed it to her, his expression bland. 'As far as I know there are one or two dinner parties—not to mention a Midsummer Ball—lined up in your honour. The acquisition of a grown-up granddaughter is not something the Earl intends to play down. And you wouldn't want him to be ashamed of you, would you?' he ended with the smooth dryness that always made Ziggy want to slap him.

Her full lower lip jutted out fractiously as she stared at the sweet she no longer had any appetite for. The first time she'd spoken to him he'd said his mother would see she had suitable clothes to wear. And he had obviously discussed her inadequate wardrobe with his parent during that phone call last night. She didn't make a habit of going round being rude to old ladies, but no way was she going to allow some insufferable, ageing county type—and any woman who had given birth to this monster just had to be insufferable—trick her up in tweeds and twinsets and the droopy chiffon which would probably be *de rigueur* for ghastly upper-crust balls! No way on God's sweet earth!

CHAPTER FOUR

'AND SO you bowed out of the domestic agency business?' Léonie asked as they left the two men to their port and gravitated to the small drawing-room—small by Staineswick standards—where the muted lighting drew warmly delicate highlights from the rose-coloured brocade upholstery that complemented the richer red of the silky carpet, the deeper tones of the sweep of velvet curtains.

'Sure. Jenny Oakes and I—she was my closest friend back at one of the schools I went to—hit on the idea and started up in a small way in Vancouver. It took off and began to look good. But the challenge had gone, for me, anyway. So I got out after Dad died.'

Even before her father's accident Ziggy had been thinking of moving on, relinquishing her share of the partnership to Jenny. She had never been easy in one place for long. There had always been a restlessness in her spirit that made the idea of settling down and committing herself to one project, one place, anathema to her. It was, she supposed whenever she'd tried to counter her mother's accusations of fecklessness, a legacy from her childhood when she and her mother had never been in one place long enough to put down real roots, following her father from one logging camp to another. It had been a way of life for Ziggy, the only life. And always, adding to the restlessness, had been the ill-defined feeling that she was searching for something...somewhere...

'And now you are here, and that is very nice for all of us,' said Léonie in her husky, slightly accented voice, moving over to the hearth with its ornately carved stone mantel, holding out her hands to the flames that threw flickering lights on to the severely beautiful linenfold panelling, and Ziggy, sinking into a plushly upholstered sofa, thought: but not nice for Rafe—then wondered why his mother, at least, didn't guess how *un*nice for Rafe her presence here must be!

Instinctively, Ziggy had taken to the older woman at once. Léonie had once been a passionately beautiful woman, she divined astutely, but all that was left now was a flamboyance of style and character that would make her worth treasuring.

'I don't think you can even begin to imagine how happy your coming here has made your grandfather.' The subject of Ziggy's thoughts sat down, the gold fabric of her flowing caftan reflecting a million glittering lights. 'When I spoke with Dudley last night on the phone he was almost incoherent about you! And I think—no, I *know*—that you and I will be great friends!'

There was a warmth of spirit about this exuberant woman that warmed Ziggy, lapped over her. Just as her grandfather had unquestioningly accepted her, so had Léonie. Unlike Rafe, they had not made her feel out of place, a nuisance, suspect. But their acceptance was, in a way, more dangerous than Rafe's implacable dislike. She could so easily succumb...

'How long have you known Grandfather?' she asked gruffly, half annoyed by her own instinctive capitulation to the friendliness of Rafe's mother. She had expected a staid dowager, resentful because a lost grandchild had been found, one who might, one day, walk away with a sizeable inheritance which would otherwise have gone to her beloved only son.

'*Mon dieu!* More years than I care to remember!' the older woman chuckled huskily. 'Many years ago he did my husband a great favour and we've kept in touch ever since. My husband was remotely related to him and we all found we had much in common. Staineswick's been like a second home to Rafe ever since he was around four years old...' Her voice tailed off as she spread her hands to the flames, her rings glinting, and Ziggy thought, so they visited, were close, at a time when no one would have dreamed that Rafe would one day inherit because the Earl still had two living sons. It turned her preconceived ideas upside down. And she said quickly, 'You must have known my father.'

'No, I'm afraid not.' Léonie's deep brown eyes were gentle. 'I met him once, briefly, at your grandmother's funeral—but those affairs are not conducive to getting to *know* a person. And later, when I brought Rafe here on a visit—he was just four years old and his father had recently died—your father had left. I'm sorry. I knew,' she continued softly, 'how grieved Dudley was when it became clear that your father had no intention of returning, and I can guess at how divided your loyalties now must be. But if you could try to look at things from your grandfather's viewpoint——'

But whatever she had meant to say was left unsaid as the door opened, admitting the Earl and Rafe, with Thurston following with the tray of coffee. Ziggy swallowed a hiss of annoyance. Whatever Léonie had been about to say might have been important. It could, perhaps, have helped to straighten out thoughts that had been growing more confused since her arrival. Nothing now seemed quite so clear-cut and straightforward as she had thought it was.

And Rafe's presence in the room was like the advent of a very large rock in a very small pool. The shock-waves crashed outwards in ever widening circles, battering at her senses, disturbing serenity, confounding her by their very forcefulness.

The disturbance, she noted giddily, was felt by no one else. The ordered pattern of movement told her that...Thurston placing the laden tray on a delicately inlaid side table, 'Will that be all, madam?' sounding like something out of an old black and white film; the Earl crossing slowly to a winged armchair, close by the hearth; Léonie pouring from a Georgian silver coffeepot, her movements relaxed, automatic, as she performed a task that must have been hers on countless evenings such as this.

Ziggy alone was touched by the silent, still presence of the smoky-eyed man whose very containment cloaked a menace that spoke only to her, and more loudly than any violent words or actions could ever have done.

She didn't understand it, this chemistry, this darkly disturbing awareness, this two-way interplay of an unknown emotion that no one else was tuned in to. And she didn't like it.

'I'll skip coffee, if you don't mind.' She got to her feet, feeling unaccountably gauche, her inner antagonism heating to hate for the man who so effortlessly made her feel stupidly childish and shallow, who diminished her self-respect, her sense of knowing who she was and what she was.

Her goodnights over, eased out of the way by the fiction of a headache, Ziggy hurried across the hall, sparing a moment to pat the two springers who rose from their night-time positions within the enclave of the chintz-covered sofas which were angled around the log fire that was kept burning night and day. And she had gained the third tread of the staircase when his incisive voice stopped her.

'A moment, Ziggy.'

She twisted round, her eyes widening, darkening with shock. Like the stag at bay, the thought bubbled into her mind, feathered with incipient hysteria. Her tactical escape had led, not to the balm of his absence, but to pursuit, the inevitable cornering of the prey.

Above her the staircase soared into the heart of the house and below her stood the man who affected her more outrageously than anyone or anything had ever done before. She questioned, 'What is it?' in a tight little voice that didn't seem like her own, and he said easily, 'Be ready to leave by eight-thirty in the morning. We have a full day ahead.'

She didn't know what she had expected, but it hadn't been anything so prosaic as this, and she echoed, 'We?' stupidly stopping to question when she knew she should have merely turned away, promising nothing, not to him, not for tomorrow, not for any time.

'You and I,' he told her patiently, shrugging a little as if he found her stupid, his wide angular shoulders not diminished one iota by the restrained elegance of the dark silk and mohair covering of the dinner jacket he wore.

'The Butterfly House first, then the grounds, the estate, the village. The whole range of Staineswick property.' His mouth angled in a smile so slight it might not have existed. 'Although it's probably not occurred to you, you have responsibilities you can't begin to guess at—or you could have, if you choose to stay here. And tomorrow I begin your education.'

His words dropped with the directness of stones into the vast silence of the great hall, a silence broken only by the soft snuffling of the dogs who had gone back to sleep, the stir of a log as it settled more deeply on to its bed of ash. And the pattering of Ziggy's heartbeats.

She did turn then, mounting the stairs which numberless unknown ancestors must have trod, reaching the dimly lit plateau of the gallery. A dozen paces to the left, then down the panelled corridor leading to her room, the door set in a pointed, arched frame. Closing it behind her, she leaned back against the smooth wood, catching her breath. She felt as though she'd run a mile. All uphill. Wondered, hopelessly, what was happening to her.

If, on the rare occasions when it had happened, she had found herself disliking a person in the past, she had been able to ignore them, never given them a second thought, got on with the important things in her life at that moment. But this man was proving impossible to ignore, to shut away in the compartment in her mind that was labelled 'Dead End'.

Ziggy heaved a sigh and walked further into the room. Someone had been in and obligingly put on the bedside light, turned back the covers. Probably one of the cream-overalled women Ziggy had come across from time to time in the corridors of the great house.

Servants. She didn't like the idea of having faceless, nameless people scurrying around to do things she could do for herself. The very idea went against the grain. Then, as she kicked off her shoes, the thought occurred that the servants, whatever, probably enjoyed what they did, and that a job—any job, in this backwoods area—was worth having. Perhaps these people even took a

warped kind of pride in working for an earl. Maybe titles
still meant something in this country.

Her skimpy cotton nightshirt had been laid out on the
pillow with as much care as if it had been fashioned in
Paris from the finest silk, and Ziggy scowled crossly.
This place, her grandfather, Léonie, were beginning to
get to her, making her see the other side of a long-held,
entrenched viewpoint.

Her father's views, which had become her own, his
antipathy towards inherited wealth and privilege, were
being gently eroded. She couldn't allow herself to stay
here for more than a couple more days. She might find
herself liking her grandfather too well, questioning more
deeply her father's viewpoint.

Time spent in the adjoining bathroom was short, her
thoughts abstracted, and she padded back to the
bedroom, clad in the cotton nightshirt, and hung her
discarded clothes in one of the immense carved oak
hanging cupboards on either side of a wide hearth which
was empty except for a great white porcelain bowl filled
with snowy sprays of lilac blossom.

The vastness of the cupboard emphasised the paucity
of her clothes. Tonight, out of deference to the for-
mality of dinner in a dining-room where as many as
eighteen chairs were ranged around a long polished oak
Jacobean table, she had forsworn her usual jeans and
had worn the only skirt she'd brought with her on this
trip to England. It was black, calf-length, in fine Indian
cotton, and she had teamed it with a passable white
cotton top, aware that the outfit didn't look up to much,
not against the setting of glittering silver and cut crystal,
of exquisite and probably priceless old china, of the
timeless masculine elegance of formal dinner jackets,
Léonie's golden flamboyance.

She crawled between the cool comfort of lavender-scented sheets, feeling lost in the hugeness of the sumptuous four-poster, and flicked off the light, staring into the darkness.

Before she slept she had to decide what to do about tomorrow. Go along with Rafe or flatly refuse to accompany him anywhere? And what had he meant when he'd talked of responsibilities? She didn't delve too deeply for an answer to that one because she had a sneaking feeling she already knew it.

She turned restlessly on her pillow, punching it. Looking out for herself was as much responsibility as she needed.

'We'll use the Range Rover.'

It was already parked on the sweep of gravel outside the main door, and Ziggy wondered if he'd been out earlier and fetched it himself. Probably not. Pressed a bell and told some minion or other to bring it round from wherever the estate and family vehicles were garaged.

But she wasn't going to let antagonistic thoughts about him spoil her day. Having decided to go along with him, rather than upset her grandfather, whose idea this jaunt had probably been, she was almost looking forward to getting to know the estate, as far as she could, in the short time remaining to her.

Rafe went down the steps ahead of her, male assurance aggravatingly evident in every movement of his jeans and light sweater-clad figure, and she followed, breathing the crisp morning air, feeling the spring sun caress her face, a hint of summer already in its fragrant breath. The morning was unused, very quiet except for the evocative call of a wood pigeon, the light whisper of wind in the tops of the newly leafing trees.

She would prefer to walk, after being cooped up in the house she needed the exercise, but he was already waiting for her by the Range Rover and he handed her in as if she were a princess, but his smoky eyes were level, brooking no argument. And she wasn't going to be the one to instigate another quarrel, was she?

Settling herself into the passenger seat, she decided primly that cool politeness would, for once, be the order of the day, as far as she was concerned, and looked around with interest at the things which must have been so familiar to her father all those years ago, as he drove around the outflung west wing of the great house, through a cobbled courtyard, a stableyard, and on down a tree-lined drive that eventually debouched into a meadow.

At the far side the sun glittered on a series of immense glasshouse roofs, on the sliding glass doors which made up the façade of the seemingly multi-purpose building, and Rafe said, a rare warmth in his voice, 'The Butterfly House. You're going to enjoy this.'

'Sure,' Ziggy said flatly, shrugging dismissively, sheer perversity making her refuse to meet him on common ground, to share anything with him, even enthusiasm, because he thought she was a trollop, ready to grab what she could, and that, in some indefinable way, threatened her, destroyed her balance, and she knew it was important that she kept her distance.

She heard the anger in his sharply indrawn breath and felt her own lungs expand, tighten, as if they no longer fitted the delicate arch of her rib cage. He gunned the engine savagely, jolting her forwards as he headed the vehicle across the meadow, slotting it neatly in front of the entrance foyer.

The word 'Sorry' hovered on her lips but was held back by a constraint unusual to her. She felt miserable, a sulky bitch, but she couldn't explain her sudden mood of contrition, nor her inability to communicate it, not even to herself, and certainly not to him.

There was already some activity in the foyer, and Rafe strode ahead, his impatient disgust with her something she felt with a sense of deep disquiet. But she would only have to suffer his disturbing presence, her own re-action to it, for another day or two, and she could manage that, just. So her smile was buoyant as she was introduced to the man who ran the place, Mike Wilson. An answering grin lit his youthfully attractive features as he came from behind a reception desk where he had been flipping through the mail and his handclasp was warmly reassuring.

'Glad to meet you at last, Miss Bellingham. We all heard you'd arrived. And I for one have been looking forward to this.'

'That I'll settle for!' The slanting eyes were deliber-ately flirtatious because she had noted the tightening of Rafe's hard face when the largesse of her smile had beamed out at Mike. So he didn't like to see her smile at this guy? Any guy? Why not? Wasn't she, as an earl's granddaughter, supposed to fraternise with the hired help?

So she would smile all the more, just for the heck of it, and when Mike said, 'I can show Miss Bellingham round, Rafe, if you've other things to do,' Ziggy tucked her arm through Mike's, the big bright smile lighting her eyes with devilry, and waved an airy, long-fingered hand,

'Sure, go back to bed, or get the valet to press your suits, or drink champagne—or whatever it is that fledgling earls do in the mornings. Mike and I can manage just fine.'

He didn't go, of course he didn't. Ziggy had always considered herself to be a lucky person, but no one could get that lucky! He was with them all the way, big, dark and brooding, his very silence a shriek of suppressed fury.

Mike too was quiet at first, and because Ziggy felt sorry that her rudeness to Rafe had probably embarrassed him, she set out to charm. It wasn't difficult, she'd been unconsciously charming all and sundry since her cradle days, and Mike was nice. He didn't make her confidence wobble, or make her feel as if she weren't nice to know.

Real enthusiasm carried her through the gift shop, the restaurant and the video room where a touch of a button produced a film and sound commentary on the theme of conservation, the way the balance of nature was being destroyed by the indiscriminate use of pesticides, then going on to show the amazing life cycle of the endangered butterflies.

But interest turned to delight as they entered the vast heated glass dome of the Butterfly House itself. She forgot Rafe's silent, seething presence as the warmth enfolded her, made special with the scent of the lush flowering vegetation, the gentle splash of water and the liquid sound of birdsong—canaries, finches, budgerigars.

Butterflies, some with as much as a seven-inch wing span, and every colour under the sun, fluttered above and around her on silent, perfect wings. Her slanting eyes were soft with pleasure as she breathed, 'Oh, this is just perfect! Where do you get them all from?'

'They come as pupae from breeding farms all over the world,' Mike grinned down at her, enjoying her delight.

'But we do breed some of our own stock, where we can. I'll show you the emerging cages later.'

Chattering, asking endless questions, Ziggy kept close to Mike's side, careful where she put her feet because stray butterflies were drinking from the pools of water which had collected on the gravel paths after the early morning watering necessary for the plants and the humidity.

The paths meandered between the lush plantings of sweetly scented jasmine and heliotrope, mimosa and passionflowers where a myriad flame-coloured Flambeaux fed and fluttered. Gravitating at last to the rocky edge of a sheet of water where goldfish swam lazily beneath the opaline buds of waterlilies, Ziggy brushed the sleeve of her apple-green tracksuit over her per-spiring forehead, and Mike pulled a sympathetic face.

'We keep the House at around eighty to eighty-five degrees, but it's the humidity that gets to you until you grow used to it. Most visitors go outside to cool down after about half an hour, have a cold drink, then come back in here.'

'Sounds like a good idea.' Ziggy was all for a stroll outside. She could cool down and look at the container plants she'd noticed, those specifically sold for English gardens, to attract native butterflies. And she could have a long, cold drink in the restaurant, which would be open by now, then come back among the exotics again.

But she hadn't bargained for Rafe. And that had been very unwise, she conceded as she felt her arm taken in a painful, determined grip before she'd even finished telling Mike she'd see him back here in about half an hour.

Visitors' cars were already beginning to arrive as she was marched out into the cooler air, so she didn't put

up more than a token show of resistance as he bundled
her into the Range Rover. She didn't want to attract more
attention than was already coming her way. But, 'I want
to——' she began heatedly as he joined her, already
starting the engine, revving it noisily, and he cut her off,
grating,

'You want this—you want that! You won't do this—
won't do that!' His foot pressed hard on the accelerator
and they screeched away. 'You are nothing but a spoiled,
ill-mannered, unpleasant brat!'

A muscle was jerking at the side of his jaw and his
skin was almost grey with anger. Ziggy averted her eyes
hurriedly. She stared ahead, her mouth compressed, her
stomach churning.

He did have every right to be livid, she admitted wryly.
She had been impossibly rude back there, and when he'd
calmed down enough to listen she would apologise. Their
verbal sparring matches had made the adrenalin flow,
almost enjoyably, now she came to think of it, but this
morning she'd gone too far. So she would apologise.
She wouldn't crawl, no, sir, but she would admit to being
wrong, and leave it at that.

They were heading for the tree-lined drive, bumping
and lurching over the meadow, and if Rafe was so mad
at her that he was taking her back to the house, and not
on a tour of the estate, as he'd said, then that was fine
by her. Just fine. She had no more desire for his company
than he could have for hers.

But part-way along the drive he swung the vehicle on
to a side track, savagely crashing through gears as he
took the steep gradient through thickening woodland,
on and on until he eventually slammed the brakes on,
bringing them to a juddering halt.

Without looking at her, or saying a word, he leapt out and was at the door at her side in moments, wrenching it open, pulling her out, and only the iron grip of his hand prevented her from falling on her knees in the thick undergrowth.

Ziggy's eyes flew up to his, alarm widening the pupils until only a rim of piercing blue remained. She dragged in a rapid breath, her heart rattling against her ribs. He didn't look calm enough to hear that apology—his eyes held murder, glittering murder—so Ziggy said nothing, discretion, for the first time in her life, holding a certain appeal. But Rafe said it all.

'I've had it up to here with you!' He drew a succinct hand across his throat. 'You've been bitching at me from the first time we met in Covent Garden. That was before you knew I'd stepped into your sainted father's shoes as your grandfather's heir, and God knows it's been getting worse ever since. It's got to stop!' He crashed a balled fist into the trunk of a tree, and Ziggy's eyes widened with alarm.

'Not for my sake,' he continued through thinned lips. 'I can take it, but for the sake of your grandfather. Lord knows why, but he already thinks the sun rises and sets with you, and I don't want to see the hurt in his eyes when you finally disillusion him. Because you make it obvious that you can't stand the sight of me and he'll notice, and he'll ask why, and you won't be able to resist spilling your poison and he'll see you for the greedy tramp you are!'

He drew in a long breath through flared nostrils and his mouth was grim. 'And I don't want to see that happen, because both his sons, in their different ways, gave him as much grief as any man can be expected to bear. So why don't you do as your father and uncle did, deny your responsibilities and get the hell back where you came from!'

'You'd like that, wouldn't you?' Ziggy flashed, anger making her stomach churn. 'That would really hurt him—but you know that, don't you? I walk away, like my father did, so Gramps disinherits me and you stand to come into everything. Very neat!'

'Were you born a cynic?' Rafe remarked drily. 'Or did your father bring you up to be like him?'

And that did it! It truly did!

'You don't know anything about Dad! You're not even fit to speak his name! You—you pompous creep!' Her voice rose with temper. 'And if you think I'm going to slope away, leaving the field clear for you, you can think again!' Her dilated eyes registered the sudden flash of fury that darkened his own, and she heard the uneven rasp of his breathing. And here, in this dense silent woodland, she felt afraid for the first time in her life.

The very last thing she would ever do would be to hang around here in the hope of financial gain, but Rafe wasn't to know that, and she was darned if she'd go away just to suit him! She had sniped at him all along the line, and although he'd said he could take it, was only concerned because of the effect her antagonism could have on the Earl, she knew he'd been lying. It was there in his eyes, in the rigid stance of his body, and she knew that her last taunt must have hit home, been one taunt too many.

The wind rustled, a menacing sigh that ruffled the dark eaves of the wood, and Ziggy turned coward for the first time ever, turned abruptly, and fled, putting as much distance between herself and the hateful Rafe d'Anjou as she could.

*   *   *

'He's in the rose garden,' said Léonie, then added quickly, 'Is anything wrong?' seeing the decisive jut of the pointed chin, the storm threat in the tilted azure eyes.

'Not a thing,' Ziggy lied. Only that when she saw that foul d'Anjou again she would kill him! But she couldn't tell his poor mother that. She was great. His father must have been a swine, though, he must have inherited his hatefulness from somewhere. 'I just wanted a chat with Grandfather,' she supplied as levelly as she could.

'This is the quickest way.' Léonie put the bunch of pink and white tulips she had just cut down on a table in the garden room where Ziggy had run her to earth. 'I've just left him sunning himself.'

She led the way down a dim corridor to a wide, oak-boarded door which opened on to a flight of shallow stone steps,

'Down the walkway and turn left as you go under the yew arch—and tell him it's almost time for tea, would you?' Her smile was pleasant, uncomplicated, but there was a shadow in the deep brown eyes. 'Don't let him get chilled. I worry about him, like a child.'

Ziggy could understand that, the friendship was old and obviously valued, and if it weren't for that fly in the ointment, the hateful Rafe d'Anjou, she would have been happy to stay on here, for a month or two even, getting to know them both.

As it was, she would leave tomorrow. No way could she and Rafe d'Anjou share the same roof—no matter how enormous that roof might be!

Despite what she had said to the contrary—just to needle him—she had no intention of staying, even if it did mean the loss of her own inheritance. She had never wanted it, anyway. But she didn't want to announce her imminent departure in a way that would hurt her grandfather. Rafe had said one true thing, the Earl had been hurt enough. And another thing had become quite clear, there were two sides to every story, and her father hadn't had right entirely on his side.

The long walk back from the woods—she had lost her way repeatedly, sheer temper making her unable to think intelligently enough to follow the right track—had done nothing to ease the fulminating rage that Rafe d'Anjou had bludgeoned to life. She hadn't come all the way across the Atlantic to be taken to task by some chinless wonder! Only he wasn't a chinless wonder, that was the trouble. He was too damned attractive for his own good. *Or for hers?* The thought sprang, unwelcome, and she pushed it away.

For her grandfather's sake she would try to behave as though that scene in the woods had never happened because he, for some crazy reason, actually liked the guy! She drew in a deep breath as she passed beneath the thick shade of the ancient, clipped yew arch and plastered a smile on her face as she turned the corner and saw the Earl sitting on a bench in the sun, overlooking the small formal garden, a silver-headed cane at his side.

The look of pleasure that lit his lined face when he saw her was enough to make her heart lurch. Without knowing how it had happened, she had actually grown fond of the old man. Something in her responded to something in him. Which was confusing, because she'd come here all set to have a grim showdown with him. But he had told her his side of the story, and his regret, his self-recrimination, had been real. She had to respect him for that.

'Come and join me,' he invited, and Ziggy sat on the seat beside him and tried to look relaxed, which was difficult because she was still seething at the things Rafe had said.

'Is something worrying you?' Astute, kindly eyes searched her almost classically beautiful little face, noting the tense line of her slender shoulders. 'You're not regretting having come here?'

Ziggy's eyes widened with the sudden impact of self-knowledge and she answered honestly, 'No, I'm glad I came. I'll always remember it all—the house, you, Léonie. Only——' she chewed on her full lower lip, searching for words '—only none of it seems quite real.'

'It's real enough,' he smiled drily. 'Real, expensive to maintain—a burden, if you like. But it's part of the nation's heritage, an irreplaceable part. And we, the Bellinghams, are merely custodians. And that's why we all work and worry and scheme and contrive and carry that burden.'

He clasped his hands over the head of his cane, the eyes that were so like her father's regarding her compassionately.

'When I die Staineswick will become partly your responsibility. The title will go to Rafe, as I believe you know, and the house and the entailed property. But the farms—seven of them—most of the village and a sizeable amount of cash will go to you. Perhaps you can't grasp what that means,' he smiled gently, 'but the unentailed part of the estate is an integral part of the whole. Without it, even with the innovations such as the Butterfly House, Staineswick would die. So you see, Ziggy, in making you heir to all that—as you, as my closest blood kin, are entitled to be—I am entrusting Staineswick's future to you.'

Ziggy shifted uneasily, unconsciously repudiating all that he'd said, and her grandfather's eyes smiled with warm understanding.

'You've been catapulted into a situation you find unbelievable, and I dare say your instinct is to back away and put as many miles between yourself and this place as you can—as any sensible young person would. But sense doesn't come into it, does it, Ziggy? Because you're a Bellingham through and through, and you can't fight that. Everything else, yes, but not that. And that's why I know you will be right for Staineswick. The responsibility is a load you will carry because your heredity won't allow you to do otherwise. And if I hadn't known that I would have already altered my will accordingly.' He smiled suddenly, looking years younger, reminding her so acutely of her father that she could have wept. 'That I haven't already contacted my firm of solicitors must tell you how much faith I put in my judgement. But you won't be alone. Everyone, from Rafe himself to the youngest gardener's boy, will be working with you, because Staineswick, and what it stands for in these days of impermanence and unease, breeds a rare and precious loyalty.'

He was taking it for granted that she would stay, and Ziggy, quite suddenly, acknowledged that he might be right. His words had touched her more than he knew, had touched a responsive chord somewhere, one she hadn't known existed, making her feel that she had come home, that her former restlessness of spirit had been leading her here, although she hadn't known it.

He had said he had faith in her, and something like that couldn't be dismissed or tossed aside.

Sudden tears sparkled on her lashes as she mentally shouldered the burden he had placed on her back. But her small, pointed chin came up in the determined fashion that was uniquely her own as she angled herself into the corner of the bench, facing him, speaking her mind as she warned him,

'Rafe wouldn't like the idea of my working with him, even for the good of Staineswick. We rub each other up the wrong way.' And that was putting it mildly! 'If he thought he'd have to share Staineswick with me he'd run a mile!'

Or make good and sure I did, and never came back, she added mentally, knowing now that Rafe's antagonistic treatment of her had been carefully planned, right from the start, with just that aim in mind.

'And in any case,' she went on waspishly, 'I wish you'd stop talking as though you were about to kick the bucket!'

'I have no intention,' the old man grinned, 'of doing anything of the sort for quite some considerable time yet! I'm tough, I've had to be, and your coming has given me a new lease of life. You're so like your grandmother, in spirit as well as in looks——' his eyes clouded briefly, looking into the past, then he shook his head, smiling again. 'You have your father's independence, but you have her spirit—and her rare beauty. And it's just as well you know what lies in front of you, don't you think? You'll need time to absorb, to adjust. And as for Rafe running a mile, you're wrong there. He's never yet run from anything. And if sparks fly between the two of you then that makes life more interesting!' He got to his feet, a speculative glint in his eyes. 'Time for tea, I think,' and Ziggy joined him, tucking her arm through his, the smile he suddenly gave her making her uneasy.

Sparks did fly, there was no doubt about that! But interesting? Hardly!

CHAPTER FIVE

ZIGGY was curled up in the wide window seat, staring blankly over the rooftops of Mayfair. She wondered if her grandfather paid for the upkeep of Rafe's spacious penthouse flat. If so, it must be a considerable drain on the Staineswick estate, she thought acidly.

She had been having a lot of acid thoughts during the seven days since she had mentally capitulated to the demands of her future, as her grandfather had spelled it out. All of them centred on Rafe d'Anjou.

She wriggled on the soft, red-upholstered cushion, absentmindedly getting more comfortable, her long jean-clad legs crossed, her knees drawn up to her chin.

Since their fight in the woods when he had told her to get out and go, she had hardly seen the monster. And when she had he had looked right through her. Like last Saturday when she'd tagged on to one of the guided tours of the house...

Not all the rooms were shown, just the state rooms and those not used by the family. It had been fascinating; Hester Povey had all the facts at her fingertips and had made the chequered history of her family come alive. She was certainly an asset, Ziggy decided as they all stood in the immense salon and Hester, in her pleasant clear voice, recited, 'In their day the Bellinghams were astute collectors; most of the French furniture you see here was acquired at knock-down prices from émigrés after the French Revolution. And the Dutch paintings came as part of the dowry at the marriage of the fourth

Earl to the daughter of a wealthy Amsterdam merchant.
In the list of the items the Dutch bride brought with her,
a Rembrandt is mentioned but, sadly, there's no trace
of such a painting now. We imagine it was sold when
the estate was expanded and vast tracts of land bought.
However,' her smile encompassed the knot of avidly
listening tourists, 'if any of you should spot it among
the other paintings, the present Earl would be most
grateful.'

There was a rustle of polite laughter, and Ziggy's
attention wandered from Hester's anecdotes, all her attention on the guide. What age was she? she wondered.
Thirty? Thirty-one? That was perhaps giving her the
benefit of the doubt, but at twenty, Ziggy could afford
to be generous. Hester was very lovely, though, a clear-
skinned ash-blonde who moved and spoke and dressed
as the very rich did.

The murmuring group of sightseers moved out on to
the gallery. The tour had ended and at the foot of the
stairs the group dispersed, chattering like children let out
of school, some to have tea in the restaurant that had
been erected in a converted stable block, others to walk
or drive over to the Butterfly House.

Ziggy hovered, intending to introduce herself to
Hester, but Rafe emerged from the room he used as an
office and for Hester, obviously, no one else existed. So
Ziggy watched, wry-faced, as Hester hurried over to the
tall dark man, tucking her arm through his, lifting a
radiant face, and Rafe said something, his eyes smiling,
as they walked deeper into the house.

They looked right together, much of an age, and would
have similar backgrounds and interests, and Ziggy wondered whether, at long last, Rafe had found the woman
he'd be prepared to tie himself down to. She would be

a great help, an asset, when he took over the reins of
the great house himself. Ziggy felt sorry for Hester.

Two days later Léonie had dropped a minor bombshell. Rafe was driving them to London and they—she
and Ziggy—would stay with him in his flat in Mayfair,
and while he went about his business she and Ziggy
would shop for clothes.

And, much to Ziggy's secret amazement, it had been
fun. Léonie's taste didn't run to tweeds and twinsets,
after all, and Ziggy had put aside all her earlier reser-
vations, seeing that if she were to stay at Staineswick
and be introduced to all and sundry as heir to a
considerable part of her grandfather's fortune, she would
need more than the jeans and T-shirts she had brought
with her.

And as for the expenditure, Gramps had barked on
seeing Ziggy's hesitancy when the trip had first been
suggested, she was to think no more of it. He had been
deprived of the pleasure of making her gifts for the last
twenty years. He now intended to do a little catching
up. He would be staying at Staineswick, of course,
London had little appeal for him these days, and much
as he would miss them they were not to return until Ziggy
had every last thing she needed.

No one but Ziggy had caught the cynical twist of
Rafe's mouth.

And now the early morning quietness of the penthouse was intense. Mrs Tranter, who kept the place clean
and aired in Rafe's absence and came in and cooked
when he was in residence, hadn't arrived yet. Léonie was
still sleeping and Rafe could be anywhere.

Since he had driven them down they had hardly seen
him; Léonie had murmured something about business
commitments and Ziggy had diplomatically kept her vit-

riolic thoughts to herself. No doubt his so-called business commitments had more to do with painting the town red than anything else. As far as she could tell he had never done a stroke of real work in his over-privileged life.

She rested her cheeks on her updrawn knees, her hair forming a shimmering raven cloak around her as her slanting eyes weighed the constrained luxury of the room. The three-bedroomed apartment was quite something, and in here the deep chairs, upholstered in smooth grey suede, the thick white carpet, spoke of impeccable taste—and no expense spared. Had Rafe demanded the place as his due? Somewhere to come when the quiet idleness of his days at Staineswick, his role as the dutiful and affectionate heir apparent, began to pall? And had her grandfather, because both his sons were lost to him and Rafe was his heir, given everything asked of him?

Ziggy wasn't sentimental, and much as she had, rather reluctantly, grown to love Staineswick she knew that holding it together for future generations wouldn't be in the least bit romantic—more like long years of solid hard work, laced with worry!

Her sessions over the last week with her grandfather and Arnold Grice, the estate manager, had opened her eyes to just how much hard work was involved. There wouldn't be a place for expensive passengers—and into that category went Rafe d'Anjou with his overbearing, autocratic manner, his expertly acquired air of breeding, his misguided opinion that the world in general and Staineswick in particular owed him a living!

But he was the future Lord Staineswick, so what could anyone do about it? Ziggy understood the frustration that had driven her father away.

A knot of something hard and hot formed inside her, just under her ribs, and it spread, lapping through her entire body as she recalled just how insufferable he was, how unfit to take her father's place! She would never forgive him, ever, for the things he'd said to her, the way he'd tried to make her feel like a common, greedy tramp, how he'd told her to go and never come back.

The door opened silently and he was there, his sudden presence sending the usual shock-waves that now froze her, scrunched up as she was in the window seat, only the deep flash of sapphire in the slanting, black-fringed eyes indicating that she was not a creature carved from stone.

He was wearing black. Black tailored slacks, a black silk shirt, and his eyes, at this distance, beneath those level dark brows, looked black too. Black and cold and fathomless, his mouth a straight, uncompromising slash, the character lines at either side deeply scored.

The indefinable aura of menace that surrounded him, reaching its threatening tentacles out to grip her in icy talons, was a tangible thing. It had been there the very first time she had seen him. She hadn't understood it then, and still didn't. And how could she—free, independent and capable of holding her own with anyone—feel threatened by such as he, an idle playboy with delusions of grandeur and very few scruples, if his treatment of her was anything to go by. He might be the future Earl of Staineswick, but it was a title that meant nothing, because without the property she would inherit, Staineswick would die. Gramps had said so and she believed him.

Rafe moved further into the room, fracturing the spell that had made the passage of those last silent, scrutinising seconds seem like eternity, a void, inhabited by only the two of them.

'There's fresh coffee in the kitchen. I've just made a pot.'

At his mundane words a deep, releasing shudder coursed raggedly through her and the spell was broken and she was able to move, untangling her legs, standing up and shaking the glossy fall of her hair back from her face, noticing for the first time that he cradled a mug of coffee in one hand, then she saw his eyes assess her in slow appraisal.

'Still nothing to wear? Even after all the hours you and Léonie spent shopping? I expected to see you trigged up in ermine and pearls!'

There was open amusement in the cultured voice, echoed by the lazy flick of the eyes that took in the shabby, hip-hugging jeans and cinnamon cotton top she wore.

Ziggy shrugged carelessly, her bare toes curling in the deep pile of the white carpet as she moved to the door. She had no intention of unpacking any of the classy boxes and carriers that had arrived by the taxi-load, not until she was back at Staineswick, and she wasn't going to dignify his sarcastic comment by giving it a reply.

'Lost for a sharp comeback?' Her mute dismissal of him had brought a glint of anger to his eyes and steel fingers reached out to fasten round her arm as she passed. 'I'm glad to see you're capable of taking notice of what I told you!'

Ziggy stood quite still, feeling as though the breath had suddenly been sucked out of her body. She could have moved away now. He was no longer exerting any real pressure on her arm. But she could feel each of his fingers, separately, the warmth of them, the latent strength. She had never been as aware of anyone or anything as she was of this man.

But he'd been referring to the tongue-lashing he'd given her when he'd effectively told her to behave herself or get out, and he thought he had her beat. And if she didn't say something, right now, he'd go on thinking that, and that would be intolerable. So she said, 'Let me go,' and he did. But he didn't move and neither did she. They were very close.

His eyes were dark and serious and they seemed to ask a question, one she couldn't answer. Or maybe he was questioning himself? The look in his eyes confused her.

A pulse began to beat rapidly in her throat as she looked into his face, seeing it clearly as if for the first time, and she knew that something was happening, but she wasn't sure what. There was a deepening, a sharpening of the tension, an awareness she wasn't at all easy with—it was as if everything that had happened before had been leading to this one moment.

She tried to speak, to say something snappy, but no words would come, so she swung on her heels and walked away, her breath expelled in a long-pent-up sigh. For a while back there, something weird had happened. But she was all right now, back in control.

She went out by the gleaming mahogany door, down the softly carpeted hallway and through to the kitchen. But Rafe followed her, and her hands shook inexplicably as she poured coffee from the jug, spilling drops of the hot, dark liquid on to the immaculate marble-grained work surface.

'Like some toast? Eggs? Mrs Tranter won't be in until eleven today, so we make our own breakfast.'

Ziggy shook her head. There was a huskiness, almost a hesitancy, in his voice. She couldn't place it. He was trying to be pleasant, acting as though nothing had ever happened between them before, and that would have been OK with her, only she could pick up that thread of something strange behind his innocuous words.

'What are you doing today? More shopping?' He put two slices of bread in the toaster, and she shrugged, looking at him over the rim of the mug she held to her mouth with both hands.

'The shopping's all done. Maybe I'll go sightseeing— I don't know. Léonie's spending the morning in bed, she said so last night. The last two days have worn her out.'

If he could be pleasant, try to batten down that ever-present antagonism, then so could she. Up until now she hadn't known how she would spend today. She still wasn't sure, but she wasn't spending it here, with him, no matter how equable he was being. That she *was* sure about.

'Then how about seeing the sights together?' He was pouring himself more coffee, not looking at her. 'I know my way around London better than you, and we could have lunch at——'

'No.' Ziggy had finished her coffee and she padded over to rinse her empty mug at the sink, and flinched as she heard the sharp clatter of the coffeepot as he banged it down on the counter. And her own mug dropped from her fingers, shattering into the sink as he took her by both arms, wrenching her round, sending her hair swirling around her head.

'You never learn, do you?' His icy eyes raked her stormy face, and she saw the hot glow of anger there. '"No" *what*?' he grated, his meaning clear, very clear, and she stopped wriggling.

'No, *thank* you!' she spat, her eyes glittering fury. 'And stop manhandling me!'

But he only pulled her closer, so close that she could feel his body heat, and it was like a sudden jolt of electricity. 'Not until you learn to keep a civil tongue in your head!'

Again the raking, angry eyes took possession of her face, and it felt as if Rafe were possessing her, and she wanted to hurt him. She didn't know why, she only knew she did. And she forced her lips to move, made her voice soft, injected a little-girl stammer.

'I'm—I'm so sorry, Rafe. Honestly.' The tip of her tongue flicked, cat-like, over her lips and she lowered her silky lashes demurely, putting on the act of her life. 'But I'll have to say no, thank you, I'm afraid. It was nice of you to offer——' She felt the pressure of his hands relax slightly, flicked up her eyes and was gratified to see a small puzzled line appear between his eyes, as if he couldn't bring himself to believe the evidence of his ears, then she carried on sweetly, 'But I really don't need you to give up your time to squire me around.' Her voice lost its sugary sweetness and dropped to a low growl. 'Because believe me, I wouldn't be seen *dead* on the streets with you!'

She felt the way his whole body stiffened, his hands tightening painfully on her arms, and her eyes flew wide open as he ground out, deep in his throat,

'You damned witch!' And then he kissed her.

It was like nothing she had ever experienced before and, for a few breathless moments, she was too stunned to do anything about his savage, wicked plundering of her mouth. His hard lips were marauding, forcing hers apart, his arms crushing her remorselessly to the steely length of his body.

Summoning all her strength, she raked at his face, her fingers like claws, but he subdued her with effortless mastery, his hands a vice around her head.

Ziggy's breathing quickened unbearably and she knew her wild struggles were only serving to increase his body's demands, and she instinctively made herself go limp.

But inside her breast her heart was beating a demented tattoo and she was trembling, her lips bruised and throbbing beneath his hard mouth. Her hands raised to strike him again, obeying the frantic prodding of her brain, but without a conscious thought they curled around his shoulders instead, obeying something deeper, more primitive than brain function.

She heard herself sigh, as if the sound came from someone else, and her eyes closed in blind reaction to her body's sudden drugged surrender.

Rafe's mouth was gentler now, the subtle movement of his lips and tongue erotically sensual, and she knew she was lost in a vortex of hitherto unknown sensation as his hands moved to her breasts, shaping them, sliding down to span the narrowness of her waist, then lower still to press her hips more deeply into the hard thrust of his loins.

She could hear his ragged breathing, a counterpoint to her own, and she knew she was drowning in strange uncharted waters, knew that she had to rely on the tattered shreds of her own willpower because she didn't think she could rely on his.

Already his lips had left her mouth, were trailing a pattern of exquisite sensation along the arched length of her throat, and desperately then, using every scrap of her strength, she jerked savagely away from him, then felt the blaze of inexplicable tears dance in her eyes, as if the brutal severance had hurt.

Flinging him an uncomprehending look, she scrubbed the back of her hand over her swollen lips, fighting the painful sob that was trapped in her chest, then turned and ran from the room on legs that felt distinctly wobbly.

Rafe had looked so strange when she had fled the room, his eyes fever-bright, his mouth a hard, savage line— only the spasmodic jerking of a muscle at the side of the strong jaw belying the coldness of those compressed, emotionless lips.

All day long images of those frenzied moments in his arms, when her body had surrendered to the heated demands of his, had entered her mind, unbidden, unwanted. And now, sitting with an untouched glass of lemonade on the table in front of her, she allowed her thoughts full rein, unable to fight them any more.

After a day of aimless wandering, getting lost and not caring, she had ended up in Covent Garden, hoping an evening with her old friends would take her mind off Rafe. She would say, 'Let's go back to Bethnal Green, we'll pick up some Chinese takeaway for supper, my treat,' and they could talk over old times and she'd tell them her news, and they might sympathise and they might beg her to go back, take up her place in the troupe. And after that kiss she might just think about it.

They were beginning their last act of the day, a new mime routine, one she hadn't seen before. It was good, very funny—but there was a new member, a girl with soft blonde hair, and with a sudden sense of depression Ziggy knew her friends, however willing, wouldn't be able to help her.

Her life with the troupe was over and done with. There could be no going back, not even for an evening. She would be returning to Staineswick tomorrow with Léonie and Rafe and she would say the words she had so far carefully withheld: 'I will stay, Gramps, learn all I can, do what I can for Staineswick, because you were right, it's in my blood.' Gramps had said he trusted her, and she couldn't deny that trust.

Even though part of her had known she would stay she had still felt a measure of freedom, of choice. Her silence on the subject had given her that. Saying the words out loud would commit her utterly, and tomorrow she knew she would say them.

Her eyes were on the antics of the troupe, but she wasn't seeing them. She was seeing the look in Rafe's eyes as she'd faced him, scrubbing the back of her hand over her mouth. It had been a childish, futile gesture. Nothing could erase the way his kiss had felt. Before, when her insults had driven his control out of sight, he had treated her like a wilful child, hurled insults in his turn. She knew now that they had cut deep, hurtingly deep.

But this morning's punishment had been far more effective. He had kissed her, used her like a woman, awakening her to a blind, unreasoning reaction, turning the coin to show the other side of hate.

She had been kissed before, but never like that. Never with the mastery that had demanded, and achieved, such a surging, melting, heated response. Before, she had always been the one in control, the one to set the pace. Past kisses had been bestowed by boys, but Rafe was no boy and his sensual expertise was unquestioned, and his shattering good looks, his lean, hard man's body, combined to make him sexually irresistible. And he probably knew it.

So she would have to tread warily, put a curb on her wicked tongue, because his new method of punishment was far more humiliating than his old one. How it would amuse him to see her melting in his arms, losing all control. His brand of kisses could become addictive, and no way was she going to allow her body's new-found sensuality to make her a slave to an arrogant, handsome, idle playboy!

'Hey—great to see you again!' Sam's hand dropping heavily on to her shoulder, nearly made her part company with her skin. She had been miles away, in a different world. 'Kate spotted you first, half an hour ago.'

'Hi!' Kate came up, grinning and running her fingers through her hair, her professional make-up looking crude close to. 'How's things?'

'Fine.' Ziggy smiled stiffly, finding it an effort. Now she was here, talking to them again, she didn't know what to say. So much had happened, so much had changed. She wasn't the same person, and she didn't know why she'd come here. And when Damien, his face closed and unsmiling, walked up to her table and said, 'You can't just walk back and expect things to go on as they were, we've already replaced you,' she merely shrugged, widening her eyes.

'I wouldn't want to. Sorry to spike your guns.'

She got to her feet and said, 'Sorry, Kate, but I've got a date,' when Kate, with a repressive glare at Damien, invited her back to share their evening meal. She had to get back to the flat in Mayfair, to begin her final adjustment to her future, to figure out, if she could, the best way of dealing with Rafe, of fathoming out—if remotely possible—how they could work together for the good of the estate.

He had become more of a problem than she had ever meant him to be. He filled her head. And this morning's explosion of sexual awareness had made him dangerous.

She had felt, right from day one, that he threatened her. And now she knew why.

Somehow she was going to have to find an inner strength, a wisdom, that would enable her to put him firmly and finally in his place. And that place was most definitely not under her skin!

CHAPTER SIX

'LÉONIE'S gone back to Staineswick.'

'Why? When?' Ziggy faced him warily, noting the lines of strain around his mouth, and he answered her drily.

'You wouldn't have to ask if you'd been here. Where were you?'

'Out.' She didn't have to account to him, not him. Her chin came up defiantly, but she thought better of antagonising him again, after what had happened this morning. And apparently Léonie wasn't here to put a damper on her son's brand of passionate punishment.

'I got lost a few times. I'm sorry I'm so late,' she elaborated cagily, although it wasn't really late, only just seven, and she would have been a heck of a lot later if she'd done as she'd originally intended and spent the evening in Bethnal Green. 'I'll go and pack my things.'

She was almost at the door, on her way to her room, wondering why on earth Léonie had taken it into her head to leave so abruptly when they could have all driven back together, when Rafe's voice stopped her in her tracks.

'No mad hurry now. We won't be leaving until tomorrow, as planned. Léonie went because there was a message from Staineswick. They'd had to get the doctor out to your grandfather, and she wanted to be with him. I put her on a train and Thurston met her and drove her home.'

'Oh, God!' Ziggy felt the colour drain out of her face and her hands flew up to her cheeks as if to contain the draining of blood. 'We must go too!'

She stared at him with anguished eyes, shocked by the depth of her reaction to the news. She had known Gramps for such a short time. How was it possible for her to love him so much? And she did love him—her reaction to the news had brought that sickeningly home to her. 'Was it another heart attack? How is he now? Have you heard? We must go—at once!'

Her knees were shaking, as if they were about to crumple beneath her, but she made a determined effort to get to her room, to throw her things in a bag—only the things she'd brought with her—the clothes she and Léonie had bought could be collected later. She didn't much care what happened to them now. They had to get back to Staineswick, to Gramps. But Rafe's hands, surprisingly gentle, stopped her, sliding down her shoulders to her upper arms, turning her to face him.

'Ziggy, he's fine.' His dark eyes were clouded, looking as if she'd just dealt him a body blow, and not the other way around. 'You care,' he said softly, almost triumphantly, 'you really do.'

He held her eyes with his, forcing the truth through the barrier of her shock. 'Léonie and I were as worried as you are—you can imagine. I couldn't go because we didn't know where you were. But Léonie phoned me as soon as she reached Staineswick, three hours ago. It had been a false alarm, Ziggy. Violent indigestion—he's as right as rain now.'

'Are you sure?' Her voice was a strained whisper as her eyes searched his, and when he nodded she sagged with relief, grateful that he was holding her. Happy to let his arms tighten around her as he drew her to the rock-solid hardness of his body. And the warmth of him, the strength of him, was suddenly, unquestioningly necessary to her now. Tears were falling, but there was heady laughter too, bubbling inside her, and her voice was growly as she muttered, 'You had me worried back there.'

'I realised that, clown!' Rafe lifted a hand and tilted her chin, and his eyes were smiling, warm with a look she had never seen in them before—not when he'd been looking her way. 'I'm sorry, I should have told you a different way. I hadn't realised you'd be so darned upset. Stupid of me.' His eyes roamed her face, her tear-spiked lashes, the drowning blue of her eyes, the quivering curve of her lips. And then, quite suddenly, the warmth was gone from his glance, and something different took its place, and she couldn't have moved to save her soul.

But he did. He put her carefully away from him, and if his smile was grim it found no echo in his casual words.

'Go and pretty yourself up. We're eating out tonight.'

There was no thought in Ziggy's head of digging in her heels and refusing to go anywhere with him. She wasn't thinking at all. Just wallowing in the relief that Gramps was all right, that Rafe had been kind when he'd seen how the news had upset her. He'd held her, comforted her, and it had felt good.

Luxuriating in the deep warm bath, liberally scented with something exotic she'd found in a cut crystal jar, Ziggy could hear him moving around in his own bathroom, crossing the hallway to his bedroom. But her mind wasn't dwelling on him as it had been all day, brooding about the way he'd insultingly manhandled her, kissed her. It was as if the inside of her head had been washed clean, emptied of everything except the relief of knowing Gramps was all right. She had lost a father and found a grandfather, and the thought of possibly losing him too, so soon, had devastated her.

Back in her bedroom, wearing a towel, she tugged a long robe of amber silk from a carrier and slipped into it. She hadn't intended wearing any of her new things until she was back at Staineswick, but tonight she felt in a mood for celebrating.

The robe felt good, trailing to the floor, the soft belt looped around her waist, the silk sensuous against her delicately perfumed skin. But she stared helplessly at the mound of boxes and carriers, wondering what to wear for dinner with Rafe.

'Pretty yourself up,' the man had said. Formal or informal? She just didn't know, and he hadn't told her. She had plenty of options, though. There were coloured separates by Lanel, a duo of elegant Conran suits, classy Jaeger casuals and a dream of an evening gown that even now made her shudder when she remembered the size of the cheque Léonie had written. And more shoes and lingerie than she thought she could ever wear—even if she lived to be a hundred and nine!

A soft tap on her door found her still hesitating, lost for choice, and she called absently, 'Come in', then, after a strange little silence, she looked up to find Rafe there.

Wearing a formal black jacket, black tie, he packed a punch that cut right through her abstraction and she felt unwanted colour paint her face as he leant back against the door frame, one hand negligently in the pocket of slim-fitting black trousers, his jacket parted to reveal a waistcoat that emphasised the masculine perfection of his honed physique.

Slow, smoky eyes drifted over the robe of amber silk that lovingly shaped her elegantly slender body, then lifted to linger on the long black hair tumbling around

her face, finally finding her eyes, holding them, sending
a message she didn't want to try to understand.

But all he said was, 'I've ordered a cab for nine. It's
half eight now,' and this lazily, as if there were no hurry
at all.

And as the door closed softly behind him Ziggy
thought, Ye gods! Half an hour. How does a girl match
that elegance, that style, in thirty measly minutes!

Taking her cue from the way he was dressed, she rum-
maged through the boxes, scattering tissue, her quick
fingers identifying wool and cashmere, linen and silk,
satin and lace, eventually locating the things she'd been
looking for. Underwear—mere scraps of oyster satin and
lace, tights—a whisper of silk, and the dress she remembered trying on in Harrods—a calf-length shimmer of
deep turquoise silk, hanging from a deeply cut yoke in
a million minute pleats.

Slipping it over her head, she walked experimentally
up and down the room, watched by a mirror image that
kept pace with her along the full length of the wall, an
image that looked different, hardly like herself at all.

The sumptuous fabric moved with her, discreetly em-
phasising the sinuous curves of her body with a sensuality that brought a wash of colour to her cheekbones.

A tiny frisson of pure excitement trickled through her
veins as she concentrated on pinning up the slippery mass
of her hair, and if the finished result looked a little pre-
carious it also looked exotic and very, very feminine.
Escaping tendrils marked the line of almost breath-
takingly pure high and wide cheekbones, the fragile
sweep of her long slender neck, and Ziggy nodded at
herself with approval. She'd do. Rafe wouldn't be
ashamed of her. And dressing up was fun, especially

when the clothes on hand were the best, ultra-feminine with just the right touch of sophistication.

Her clothes to date had always been inexpensive, chosen to suit her casual life-style and low budget. But now she was discovering the way wild silk felt and moved against soft female flesh, how delicate high-stepping sandals imparted a seductive line to ankle and calf that she had never noticed before.

She added a touch of make-up; just a smoky blue eye-shadow and a hint of blusher, her only jewellery the slender gold chain that never left her neck because it had been her father's last gift to her. Then a final touch of sheer nonsense—an endless feather boa, looped twice around her throat, framing her face, the trailing ends thrown over her shoulders to fall almost to her ankles.

Then she was ready, and Rafe was in the dimly lit living room, waiting, a glass of Scotch in one hand. And his eyes said it all: that she was looking good, very good, that the gamine had become a woman at last—elegant, poised, a hint of eternal female mystery in the tilt of her head, the slant of azure eyes, the slow curve of lips that hinted at secrets, not to be told, not yet.

'Ziggy——' There was a strange tautness in his smile as he put his glass down, finding the surface of the low table by instinct because his eyes didn't leave hers. His were shadowed eyes, holding a slick of unbelief, and Ziggy's heart began to dance to a sweet, wild music because, just for one moment, the hard and self-contained Rafe d'Anjou looked as if he'd been poleaxed. And it had been down to her—gawky, stringbean Ziggy, dressed in silk and making the urbane and lofty Rafe look at her as if she were, miraculously, an alluring and bewitching woman. Heady stuff indeed!

He might have said more than the two syllables of her name that seemed to have been shocked out of him, but the blaring of the taxi horn put paid to that. He looked almost disappointed for a second, then smiled, the old easy arrogance back as he said simply, 'Time to go. I hope you're hungry.'

But at the door of the flat he put his hand on her arm, cupping her elbow, and the touch of his skin on hers took her breath away. In the cab, sitting silently at his side, she thought about that. It had been nothing, she decided at last. It had to be nothing. Nothing more than the sly magic of her own transformation. Nothing at all to do with the physical magnetism of the darkly attractive man at her side, the shadowed eyes that never left her face yet told her nothing as he sat angled against the door, watching her, his thoughts his own.

He was a perfectly packaged, superb specimen, she had to agree with the evidence of her own eyes. But she knew him, and what she knew of him she didn't like. And in that lay her salvation.

But he was sexy, she acknowledged, her mouth suddenly dry. Not in the obvious way of lesser men. Not for him the choice of too-tight jeans, shirts open to the waist and gold medallions on chains. His sex appeal was subtler, and more effective for that. It surrounded him like an aura. It was just there.

Ziggy was relieved when the short journey was over. In the dusky intimacy of the taxi her new awareness of Rafe was almost painful. It made her feel slightly sick, and excited, both at the same time. And the palms of her hands felt damp.

The cabby deposited them outside the restaurant Rafe had chosen, and his hands rested on the small of her back as he ushered her beneath the discreet awning, past a uniformed doorman who saluted, said, 'Good evening, Mr d'Anjou', and into a small marble-paved foyer that had crimson walls and was lit by a chandelier, its brilliant frozen droplets hanging high in a roof space that soared to the full height of the building.

A woman in black chiffon greeted them both by name, her smile warm in a patrician face, the discreet glint of diamonds showing on earlobes that were left clear by the immaculate upsweep of silver grey hair. And seated in the romantically lit restaurant Ziggy surprised herself by not feeling out of place. In fact she felt in her element, and if this was part of the good life then she might just get to enjoy it!

Their candlelit table was in an alcove between two of the gold and black japanned pillars that were a feature of the room, quiet and secluded enough for Rafe to say mockingly, 'I don't want to create a ruckus, Ziggy, but tell me, do you get an adolescent thrill out of annoying me? Or does your dislike run deeper?'

He leaned back in his seat, his expression hard to read. 'I honestly want to know what you have against me, because when I know I might be able to put it right.'

She hadn't expected this. She had been high on relief, in the mood for celebrating, and something in his reaction to her earlier, and the memory of the way he'd kissed her that morning, had added an extra, deeper excitement, almost frightening, yet exhilarating.

And now it seemed he was ready to stage another fight! Although he had stated that it wasn't his intention, Ziggy could see no other reason for bringing up the vexed subject of their past slanging matches.

He was patiently waiting for her reply, but for once she was speechless, her tongue stuck to the roof of her mouth. She stared numbly at the candle in its smoked glass bowl between them, then into the glittering depths of her dry Martini.

Rafe was right on both counts, of course. Crossing verbal swords with him had always got the adrenalin running, but it did go deeper than that, much deeper, and there was precious little he could do to put it right, because he was as he was and nothing could alter that.

She twisted the stem of her glass and although she felt brittle with an uncharacteristic distaste for hurting him, she said slowly, pacing the words out as if to give herself time to examine them, reassess the worth of what she was saying, 'I don't believe in inherited wealth, or in people who live the good life, not having earned it, as if it were their God-given right.'

She raised her glass to her lips, the liquid sliding cool and sharp and welcome down her throat, and risked a look at him beneath heavy, fringing black lashes. But his boldly drawn features were enigmatic and he raised one brow slightly.

'And?'

'And right from the start, you, for me, have represented the epitome of all I despise. Well educated, obviously, but not using that expensive input to any useful purpose. Well heeled, affording the best because the means to do so was handed to you on a plate. Assured, privileged, superior—yet not having earned the right to be so. My father left all that behind, he worked for every single thing he had and he kept his self-respect, stood equal to—not superior or inferior——' Her words stumbled as she remembered the man she had always believed to be perfect. But no one was perfect, and he'd been wrong in not agreeing to meet his own father at least half-way...

Rafe leaned forward, tilting her chin, forcing her to meet his eyes. And his eyes were warm, understanding even, not angry as she had expected.

The touch of his strong warm fingers on her cool skin was sensationally persuasive and, as though mesmerised, her eyes dropped to the beautifully crafted male mouth as he told her,

'You say you don't "believe" in inherited wealth and privilege. But it's a fact of life, Ziggy, and you have to believe in facts.' Slowly his fingers released their hold on her pointed little chin and slid down the slender length of her throat, making her gulp, and then away, to cradle his glass, his eyes still intent on hers. 'And you, one day, will inherit part of a great property, and with it, a great responsibility. Will you turn your back and walk away? Take your money and cut and run? Somehow, I don't think so. Not now. Lately, my opinion of you has altered dramatically, and I think you're stronger than that. And if my so-called position in life is all you have against me, then you see before you a man with an easy mind.'

She eyed him warily, not understanding him, suspicious of his motives. He smiled at her, slow and certain. 'Now we've got that out of the way, we can relax and enjoy the evening.'

An almost unnoticeable movement of his hand brought a white-coated waiter over, and they chose what they'd eat together, in rare harmony, because Ziggy had decided to do as he had suggested and relax, enjoy, putting his questions, his odd final remark to the back of her mind to be thought about later. She knew, somehow, that this evening could be memorable, very special, if she allowed him to make it so.

And from then on he charmed her. She guessed it was deliberate, but she didn't let that worry her. She was content to be charmed, just for this once.

Rafe fed her delicious grains of beluga caviar on wafer-thin morsels of toast, touching her suddenly sensitised lips with the tips of his fingers. It was incredibly erotic, dangerously so, and the pale golden wine foamed in crystal flutes, and he was making love to her with his eyes. Smoky eyes, hinting, inviting, promising, till her breath was sucked backwards into her chest. She had never felt like this before, as if she were on a roller coaster gone out of control—excited, touched with fear, utterly reckless.

Every word, every look, every seemingly negligent touch, added to her original assessment of his potential danger, the threat she had sensed in him right from the start. But now she knew where the danger lay, had known it clearly since Rafe had held her, kissed her, this morning. She was intoxicated by it, by the sharp spice of danger as much as by the wine and the fine brandy they'd had with their coffee.

She was so tuned in to his presence that when he took her hand in the darkness of the cab that took them home a shudder so deep that she thought it might tear her apart raced through her, deepened intolerably by his huskily spoken words.

'When I see you, touch you, my heart soars.'

After that she was hardly aware of anything, save him, until they were in the quiet luxury of the sitting room back at his flat. Aware of nothing except that, madly, she wanted, needed, him to kiss her again. A real kiss, a giving and taking kiss, not one that was instigated by his anger and ended by her childish repudiation as this morning's had been.

This one evening had been out of step with time, a rent in the veil of what was prudent and careful. A kiss, one kiss, would be the prefect ending to an episode which had been touched by magic. An evening which, because of who they were and how they viewed each other, would never occur again.

And as if nothing could stop it, because this moment had been ordained since the second they had met, Rafe took her in his arms and she turned to incandescent flame as he kissed her, melting, moulding her untutored body to his as his lips ravished hers, moving expertly, sensually, his subtle exploration almost mind-bending.

She craved more, more of the potently sensational experience, her body, if not her intellect, perfectly attuned to his. But he released her gently, putting her slightly away, and she groaned an instinctive and revealing protest and he took her face between reverent hands, searching her eyes.

Her eyes were doorways to another world; slanting, misty with desire, unknowingly provocative, and he said, his voice deep and throaty, 'Marry me, Ziggy.'

Still cradling her face, his thumbs feathered over her lower lip, and the tip of her tongue languorously touched the warmth of his flesh, tasting it, and—almost—she could have said yes.

And if he'd taken her in his arms again she would have said yes, because the instincts of her body were stronger than her mind, but a shudder ran through him, as deep and as devastating as her own had been earlier, and he released her quickly, moving away. And she felt cold and deprived and incredibly alone.

'Go to bed, Ziggy,' he told her hoarsely. 'If you don't go now I might get us both into something you might regret. And think about what I asked. Sleep on it. And if your answer's "no" I'll go on asking. Be sure of that.'

CHAPTER SEVEN

IT WAS late when Ziggy woke. Ten o'clock, and sunlight was doing its best to penetrate the thickness of the heavy linen curtains. She stretched lazily and just for a second wondered why she felt so tinglingly alive, why a nimbus of shimmering excitement seemed to surround her. Then she remembered. Rafe. Last night. Her blind response to his lovemaking. His astonishing proposal.

She felt hot colour burn her face and then she smiled, couldn't stop smiling because she had never felt so alive, so female before. Rolling out of bed, stark naked, she looked at herself in the mirror. She looked as different as she felt, her sleep-mussed hair tumbling over her shoulders, curtaining her small rounded breasts, her eyes hazy, looking almost drugged with that strange inner excitement, her lips softer, fuller, inviting...

Even after a brisk shower her eyes still brimmed with sleepy excitement, and she wrapped herself in the amber silk robe and wondered what would happen if she went to him now and said, 'I've thought it over, and I will marry you,' and her face flamed as she pictured his response. His kiss, his touch, would sear her, and it would be wonderful. And for just a few delicious moments, until she took herself firmly in hand, she resavoured the magical sensations he had created in her last night.

But it wouldn't be like that, of course, because she would never marry Rafe. The very idea! She didn't love him. She didn't even like him. And why he had asked her to marry him, just like that, was anyone's guess.

Only it hadn't been 'just like that', had it? They'd spent a charmed evening together and the sexual awareness had been there, before that. So maybe he fancied her, but he hadn't said he loved her.

Beyond solving the enigma, Ziggy put down her hairbrush as she heard the shrill of the doorbell, followed by a light, feminine voice, Rafe's deeper answering tones as the visitor, whoever it was, penetrated further into the apartment.

Never short on curiosity, Ziggy tightened the belt of her robe and followed the sound of voices and the mellow aroma of coffee to the kitchen, and her eyes flew open as they homed in on Hester Povey, who was about the last person she had expected to see. Hester, turning, her lovely face flushed, raked a glance over the amber robe and smiled, 'Good morning, Ziggy. I hope I didn't disturb you,' and Ziggy replied evenly,

'Not at all. I overslept.'

Hester nodded. Her mouth was still smiling but her eyes were not. She'd seemed friendly enough—curious, but that was natural—when Léonie had introduced them last Sunday, after the last tour of the house. But now Ziggy scented resentment coming over, only faintly of course because Hester was well bred, but there all the same. And it found an echo in Ziggy's heart because, she had to admit, she had been looking forward to seeing Rafe this morning, and telling him that no, she couldn't marry him, but asking why he'd asked. She wondered if his reply to that would surprise her. But she'd have to wait until Hester took herself off before she knew the answer to that one.

'I was about to come and haul you out.' As Rafe handed her a mug of coffee their fingers brushed, and a sharp zip of excitement jagged through her—quite out of proportion to the simple contact—and his eyes were warm with an intimacy that turned Ziggy's knees to jelly.

She flicked him a slanting, unknowingly provocative look as she cradled the mug in long-fingered hands and thought, Boy, but he's dishy! Then chided herself for allowing the carnal to override the control that was going to be necessary from now on in her relationship with him.

She wasn't going to marry him. They would get no closer than future co-owners of the Staineswick estate, and when Hester left she would explain that to him.

Only Hester wasn't leaving. Ziggy's eyes narrowed as the older woman turned to her again, the friendliness all on the surface but something distinctly disturbing underneath.

'I came begging a lift back home. Father and I have been staying for a few days at the Victory Services Club and were due to drive back today. But Father met up with some of his old Army cronies and decided to stay on over the weekend.' She shrugged prettily, smiling softly for Rafe, her eyes dewy now with none of the coldness that had been there when she'd looked at Ziggy. 'I was on my way to Euston when I remembered Rafe would be driving back today.' Again the melting look for the tall, dark man who today, Ziggy noted sourly, was looking as devastating as ever in a hip-clipping pair of tailored slacks and a crisp white cotton-knit sweater. 'I do hope I'm not being a nuisance?' Hester fished with a self-deprecating dip of her head.

'I'll get dressed.' Ziggy clomped her half-empty mug on the table and removed herself swiftly. She didn't know which she resented more, Hester's untimely arrival or Rafe's warmly denying words, 'You, my poppet, couldn't be a nuisance if you tried!'

* * *

Fuming silently in the back seat of the Rolls, Ziggy
stopped listening in on the involved conversation in the
front of the car—all concerned with estate matters which,
surprisingly, Rafe seemed to have at his fingertips as,
not so surprisingly, did Hester.

If Rafe wanted a wife, she pondered dourly, some
willing woman to provide an heir, to take the lion's share
of the workload that running Staineswick would involve
off his broad but uncaring shoulders, then he would have
been better off proposing to Hester. Hester obviously
was fully aware of that and was probably confidently
waiting for the blinkers to drop off his smoky grey eyes,
her thoughts grumbled on, in peeved fashion, through
her brain.

They were so right together, like unto like, and Hester
doted on him and so would be prepared to overlook his
lack of husbandly qualities, and she hadn't been one bit
pleased when Ziggy had sauntered into the kitchen that
morning wearing nothing but a slinky silk robe. And
she'd be even less pleased if she learned what had gone
on last night! Not that she ever would, of course. And
as for Rafe's part, he had said, and had quite obviously
meant it, that Hester couldn't be a nuisance if she tried.
While she, Ziggy, had been nothing but!

In the flurry of homecoming Ziggy's spirits lifted from
the mire they had wallowed in on the journey to
Shropshire. It was good to see Gramps again and, later,
to listen to Léonie's explanations of how worried she'd
been until she had arrived home yesterday and learned
that the Earl's chest pains had been nothing more serious and alarming than acute indigestion, and Ziggy
said, 'I know! I went into panic too,' and smiled because
they could laugh comfortably together now over what
had been a hairy experience.

Dinner that evening was a quiet affair, just the three of them, and Ziggy described the clothes they'd bought, for her grandfather's benefit.

Léonie said, 'It was fun. Shopping for lovely things makes me feel young.' The big brown eyes crinkled with laughter. 'Though I have to confess I hardly ever feel old. I'm over sixty—by how much I refuse to say—but I rarely feel a day over sixteen! Can you believe that?'

Ziggy, slicing a peach, said she could easily believe it. Léonie exuded life and laughter and heart and would never grow old in spirit. As she put down her fruit knife, her eyes glanced between her grandfather and Rafe's mother.

'Rafe not eating here tonight?' That he was not was quite obvious, but she half hoped to learn that he'd said he wasn't hungry, because she dreaded the alternative—that he might be wining and dining Hester, somewhere quiet, just the two of them. Which, she admitted to herself, was a stupid, dog-in-the-mangerish attitude to take because, after all, she didn't want him and Hester did.

'He went straight back,' said Léonie. 'He got a panicky phone call and he's getting a late flight home to Normandy. Pouf!' She raised her hands as though invoking a higher authority. 'Why can managers never manage? And why does that son of mine take every facet of life so seriously!'

And before Ziggy could ponder the disparity of viewpoint—she, had she been asked for an opinion, would have had no hesitation in stating dogmatically that Rafe took nothing seriously except his personal pleasures and wellbeing—Léonie began to babble on about the Midsummer Ball which was to be given at Staineswick, in Ziggy's honour, and to which everyone, but everyone, would be invited.

'And you, my dear Dudley, won't be troubled by any of the arrangements. I take everything to do with it on my own head! You will be consulted, naturally, but very gently, and I can promise that all will be perfect—just as you would wish it to be!' She put one hand over the Earl's and the other over Ziggy's and launched into a torrent about guest lists and musicians and who would be staying overnight, and who would not, while Ziggy, finding her grandfather's benevolent eyes on her, smiled affectionately back at him, caught up in the closeness, the togetherness of the situation, and forgot that she'd been meaning to ask just why Rafe had had to go to Normandy, of all places.

As one day rolled into another Ziggy was drawn more deeply into the life of the great house and estate. The faceless, nameless servants became real people, with their own lives and personalities, and she discovered that they didn't bow and scrape and tremble in their shoes whenever their duties brought them in contact with the Earl. They were proud of the work they did because they did it well, and were part of a family, all pulling together.

It was Arnold Grice, the estate manager, who introduced her to the villagers and tenant farmers, who explained how the rents from the properties which she would one day inherit were ploughed back into the estate, improving the tenants' homes, providing extra facilities for the village school, paying the wages—not only for the staff at the great house itself, but for the permanent team of craftsmen which was necessary to keep the estate-owned property in repair.

The income from the Butterfly House, the tours of Staineswick, the restaurant in the converted barn, went some way to keeping the fabric of the main house in repair, and Ziggy could see how the two parts of the estate meshed, and knew her grandfather had been right when he'd said that without the support of the unentailed properties, Staineswick would die. So, when she inherited, she wouldn't sell up and cut and run, as Rafe probably feared. Gramps already knew she wouldn't, she'd told him, and he trusted her, and that was all that mattered.

'I won't frighten you by trying to explain all this lot.' Arnold's weatherworn face was wry as he waved a large horny hand at the pile of mail on the desk in the room Rafe used as an office—where the two of them had lunched on her first full day here, and he'd tried to explain how the estate was run. But she hadn't wanted to listen, not then.

Now she said, 'Can I help? Please let me,' but Arnold came back quickly,

'No, bless you! I'll just deal with what's vital and the rest can wait for Rafe. He knows his way around this sort of paperwork. Been doing it long enough. I'll just phone through to my missus and tell her to keep the dinner hot. You cut along.'

So she did—pondering. From what Arnold had said, Rafe was a born pen-pusher. Had he been a humble clerk before the glad news of his elevated position had released him from that particular tedium? She didn't think so, somehow. She couldn't imagine him having spent his adult life behind a desk, immersed in paperwork.

She was still pondering this when she almost ran Léonie down. Léonie was carrying an important-looking floral arrangement, very Constance Spry-ish, which was destined for the state dining room, and she yowled

'Ooops!' and averted a minor calamity with an adroit swerving movement.

'Hester would not be pleased if we ruined her master-piece! It has taken her hours—but she does them so beautifully, doesn't she?'

Ziggy had to agree with that as Léonie placed the ar-rangement on an eighteenth-century side table where it would lighten the exclusive atmosphere of the enormous dining room and delight the tourists who would arrive in throngs tomorrow.

An elaborate epergne, holding rose-coloured sweet peas and tiny white rosebuds, already stood in position in the centre of the immense Georgian dining table, a delicate counterpoint to the Georgian silver and glass and the heavily decorated and gilded Coalport dinner service which was left in situ when the house was open to the public because the visitors liked to imagine that the Earl and two dozen or so glittering guests were about to walk in and sit down to eat and converse about all sorts of fascinating people in high places.

No, Hester couldn't be faulted in any way, Ziggy thought sourly, then, aggravated by her own meanness of spirit, she tucked her arm through Léonie's as they walked together out of the room.

'Will Rafe be back in time for the Ball?' she asked his mother, trying to keep her voice light, as if she didn't care, one way or the other. It took some doing, which was odd, because she didn't care, did she?

He had been away for three weeks already, with never a word said as to why, or for how long. But his life was his own and it didn't matter to her if he never showed his face again, and the longer he was away the sooner he'd stop haunting her dreams. For he did haunt them, damn him! And more often than not in an erotic fashion that ought to make him ashamed of himself!

'If he isn't, I'll box his ears—big as the brute is!' Laughter rippled through the mother of the brute and Ziggy laughed too, though she didn't know why. 'It will be your evening, of course.' The Midsummer Ball was four days away. 'But as the future Lord Staineswick he should be at your side. He knows that. You will need support, and Rafe's presence will take a great deal of pressure off your grandfather. Now,' Léonie squinted at her watch, 'I must hurry if I'm to make myself presentable for dinner. The exercise, though fascinating, takes longer with each passing year!' She swooped up the great staircase with an energy that mocked her years, and Ziggy padded after her.

'Léonie, why did Rafe go to Normandy? Tell me to button my lip if it's none of my business, but——'

'What a quaint expression!' Léonie came to a halt, tipping her head, her eyes alive with inner amusement. 'So you wish to know where the brute is, and what he is up to, and with whom?'

'No,' Ziggy denied quickly and untruthfully, frowning as she saw amusement turn to something that looked suspiciously like satisfaction in the watchful brown eyes.

'In Normandy, near Saint-Valéry-en-Caux, we too have the doubtful privilege of owning family estates. Do you know——' Léonie sighed and looked uncharacteristically wistful '—when Rafe's father married me he loved me enough to bow to my father's wishes—he was a dreadful old tyrant, you understand—and to take my family's name. There was no son, you see, and my father wished the d'Anjou name to continue as it has, of course, through our son, Rafe. Ah, well——' she lifted her hands in a purely Gallic gesture, 'I lost my beloved husband when Rafe was less than four years old and until our son reached early manhood I had to muddle along as best I could.' She sighed again, and Ziggy dipped her glossy black head in sympathy, only to jerk it upright again at what came next, because she most surely hadn't been expecting it.

'And then—pouf! The energy, the determination—it was incredible! That boy put every ounce of his energy into putting things right. The farms were reorganised and made to pay, the Château cleaned out from top to bottom and opened to foreign visitors. Paying guests were taken in too—those fortunate enough to be able to afford the tariff! Rafe was truly formidable, and that is why——' her generous bosom swelled with pride '—your grandfather, who knew all that my son had accomplished, of course, invited him to advise on the way Staineswick could best be made self-supporting and viable. That was a few years after young Dudley's death, when it was believed that your father would inherit.'

'And Rafe's been here ever since?' Ziggy's eyes were popping over what Léonie had revealed, and the other woman laughed throatily.

'No, no! Not all the time! He came, made suggestions—put in a lot of spadework too. Now, I would say he divides his time roughly equally between Saint-Valéry-en-Caux, Staineswick, and the few exclusive and highly prosperous nightclubs he owns in France.'

'Goodness!' Ziggy couldn't think of anything more sensible to say, and she watched Léonie walk on upwards and then sat down in the middle of the staircase, a small, lost figure, sunk in her own thoughts.

And those thoughts were pretty tumultuous. Once again she had stubbornly held on to opinions which were totally opposed to reality. Just as her grandfather was not the stern, unloving man of her earlier imaginings,

so Rafe had turned out to be as much unlike her entrenched and jaundiced view of an idle playboy as it was
possible to get!

The truth would take some assimilation, and right now
she felt too confused to begin to try, and when Jane, a
stack of clean linen held against her cream overall, called
down the stairs, 'Oh, so there you are, Miss Ziggy.
There's a phone call for you—you might as well take it
in the housekeeper's room as it's the nearest——' it was
as much as she could do to get herself together and along
to the spacious, sun-filled room where Mrs Thurston did
her accounts.

She said 'Hello' and heard someone, probably Arnold,
put an extension receiver down—probably in Rafe's
office—and a much-remembered voice said deeply,

'Ziggy. I've missed you.'

Her fingers tightened convulsively round the receiver
and her bones felt as if they'd turned to water. And all
because the man who had annoyingly occupied her mind
for three whole weeks had actually remembered she
existed!

'Not enough to get in touch before,' she answered
tartly, having just recalled that she didn't really care
whether Rafe remembered her or not and that it would
be better if he didn't, actually. 'Where are you?'

'Saint-Valéry-en-Caux. I've been busy polishing all
those silver spoons you seem to believe I was born with!
And fighting myself every time I wanted to pick up the
phone and talk to you, or felt like getting the first flight
back so that I could see you again, touch you.'

Ziggy ignored that last bit. It would do her no good
at all to dwell on such lover-like sentiments. Besides, she
felt a fool—in the light of what she'd only just learned
from Léonie. She closed her eyes and groaned inside as
she recalled how Rafe had said, 'If my so-called position

in life is all you have against me then you see before you a man with an easy mind.'

She had wondered what he'd meant, and now she knew, but that didn't make anything any easier, only more confused, and she muttered, 'Well, don't let me keep you,' and he took the breath out of her body, his voice threaded with something dark and warm. Something that sparked unstoppable excitement to immediate and vivid life.

'You've been on my mind, Ziggy, day and night. I've been desperate to get in touch but knew I had to give you more time. Have you thought about what I said? Will you marry me?'

It was some time before she could answer, and when she did manage at last to get her muddled thoughts back into some semblance of order her voice was a croak.

'No. It's a crazy idea.' And she added, when the silence from his end seemed about to burn her ears clean off her head, 'Why bring that up again? Why now?' and that did get an answer, and the words were clipped.

'Because there was no opportunity to pursue the subject, if you remember, on the following day. And because I'd hoped, for three long weeks, that your answer would have been "Yes, please", and then I could have produced a ring on Midsummer Eve and made the Ball a double celebration. But I'd forgotten your irritating habit of automatically saying "No" to everything I ask. Stupid of me, wasn't it? See you.'

The line went dead and Ziggy stared at the earpiece as if, genie-like, Rafe might materialise. When he showed no signs of doing any such thing she replaced it gently and went to her room.

She felt like crying.

CHAPTER EIGHT

ZIGGY fastened the sapphire collar around her throat with shaking fingers. It was the final touch, her grandfather's seal of approval. Earlier, he had called her to his room and had taken a flat, leather-bound box from a wall safe and had revealed the glittering jewels.

'This was one of your grandmother's favourite pieces. The stones matched her eyes. It's yours now, so wear it, for me and for her, tonight.'

The collar felt cold against her skin, but the rest of her body was burning, touched by fire, and she stepped back, surveying her party self in the cheval glass, and knew she had never looked so good—yet never felt so tense.

'Perfection!' Léonie entered the room on silent feet, looking regal in black crêpe-de-Chine, diamonds flashing at her throat and ears. 'I knew you would look sublime in that gown! How very, very right I was!'

The dress was classically simple. Heavy, dull oyster satin, as rich as cream, the long skirts falling in stiff folds, the sleeveless bodice plain but deeply veed at back and front, the stark simplicity of the costly creation drawing attention to the glossy pile of Ziggy's raven hair, the curve of scarlet lips, the sapphire of slanting eyes and gemstones.

'Perfection!' Léonie repeated, her head tilted consideringly. 'You have no need of frills and flounces to draw all eyes. And your grandmother's sapphires are exquisite on you. Now, are you ready? No butterflies in the tummy, I hope.'

There were, about a million of the fluttery creatures, but Ziggy wasn't going to let her new and elegant image down by saying so!

'A moment.' She crossed to the dressing table, the stiff folds of her skirt swaying to the elegant movement of her lithe body, and sprayed herself with cologne, closing her eyes as the drift of perfume began a light invasion of her senses.

And still she couldn't bring herself to ask if Rafe had returned. Strangely, she felt shy of mentioning his name, even in such an innocent connection. And she couldn't make up her mind as to which would be worse—seeing him again, after the phone call of the other day, or knowing he'd deliberately kept away because he wouldn't be placing a ring on her finger, as he'd said he hoped.

She had kept to the house all day, waiting and watching for him, knowing she was keeping a vigil, but not knowing quite why.

Ignoring Léonie's advice that she relax out of doors in the fresh air, she had helped the staff to put the finishing touches to the guest rooms, stood by in mute admiration as Hester had overseen the gardeners as they'd carried in freshly cut greenery and great tubs and sprays of hothouse plants until the main rooms had resembled vast conservatories.

And she'd made a point of being with Léonie when the overnight guests had arrived—those with the close connections of long-standing friendship and those who had too great a distance to travel back to their own homes tonight.

She had greeted them all, trying to remember names and faces, all the time looking for a tall, dark man with eyes like smoky grey glass.

But there had been no sign of Rafe, not even when everyone had sat down together to an early and informal light dinner.

And now, as she walked beside Léonie, along the gallery to the head of the stairs, her heart was pattering like a wild trapped thing.

'You have no need to be nervous,' Léonie assured her roundly as they descended the stairs side by side. 'Everyone will love you—how, indeed, could they fail!'

If Léonie put her silence down to pre-big-party nerves then that was all right by Ziggy. It was partly the case. She would be on show in front of over a hundred guests whose breeding would not be quite enough to prevent them from avidly sizing up the girl who was the Earl of Staineswick's long-lost granddaughter.

But pre-party nerves were only partly to blame for her fine-tuned tension, and she knew who held the lion's share of that blame by the way her jitters miraculously took immediate flight as she caught sight of Rafe's broad shoulders as he stood at the foot of the stairs. He had been talking to the butler, and now Thurston paced sedately away, nothing, not even putting Staineswick on show, not to mention the last of the direct line, disturbing his pedantic serenity.

Then Rafe turned, looking upwards, and as she noted the sudden shaft of joy that transformed his craggy features when his eyes met hers her heart swelled with a nameless emotion and she knew she was glad, glad that he had come, after all.

But the look of unguarded joy was quickly erased by the man who was an expert when it came to hiding his real feelings, and was smartly replaced by his usual slightly sardonic smile as Ziggy floated down the few remaining stairs, her own smile unstoppable because he was here, and it was good, so good, to see him. She had thought, after that telephone conversation, that he wouldn't want to have anything to do with her for a long, long time.

Then the Earl appeared at Rafe's side, as formidably elegant in his own way as the younger man, and made the courtesy of bending his aristocratic white head over Léonie's hand, then Ziggy's, and there was a distinct catch in his voice as he stated, 'Staineswick has not been so graced for many years. Too many years,' and Ziggy knew he was remembering the woman who might have been her double, all those years ago, the woman who had worn the sapphire collar, whose slanting eyes would have been warm with love for him.

Then the brief echo of sadness was gone as Ziggy pressed her grandfather's hand sympathetically, and Rafe, offering his arm to his mother, suggested, 'We've time for a quiet stiffener before the hubbub begins. In the library?'

'Damn sensible idea!' The Earl blew his nose—a defiantly trumpeting sound, yet tinged with pathos—then gave Ziggy his arm. 'Lead on, my boy! We're right behind you!'

After that brief oasis of peace, the evening began to swing into action and the great house came alive with music and light and laughter.

Ziggy, flanked by her grandfather and Rafe, greeted the arriving guests, a performance which went on for over an hour and from which Gramps, after twenty minutes or so, was discreetly extricated by Léonie.

And Ziggy, watching them move slowly away, stopping to chat briefly to this person or that, felt her head reel with the effort of smiling, of trying to fix so many names and faces in her mind.

But Rafe's hand beneath her elbow, the slight pressure of his fingers, was a wordless and welcome transmittal of strength, and she leaned against him, just slightly and briefly, and was able to switch on her most dazzling smile for a fat, red-faced old squire who goggled, flushed even more deeply and tugged at his waistcoat, then spent the rest of the evening telling anyone who'd listen that Lord Staineswick's granddaughter was a 'damn fine filly'.

For Ziggy, the evening soon became a hopeless blur; matrons with unmarried sons cornering her, pulling her into endless conversation, dancing in the ballroom—the first dance with Rafe, who held her stiffly, the regulation three inches of space between them at all times, then with a succession of others—old, young and middlish—all similarly blessed with a boring repertoire of small talk.

Gramps retired after Ziggy, the star exhibit of this Midsummer Ball, had been toasted in vintage champagne. And she had seen no sign of Léonie since, half an hour ago, that lady had advised her to send her current dancing partner for a plate of food from the lavish buffet where the variety of goodies was beyond enumeration.

'And where has Rafe got to?' Léonie had hissed as Ziggy's perspiring young partner smartly obliged, and Ziggy, her feet aching and her head swimming, had replied dully,

'I haven't seen him around for some time,' failing to add that the last time she had seen him he'd been dancing with Hester, and there hadn't been a millimetre of space between them, let alone three inches.

That had been when she'd started to feel headachy and dispirited. His tanned cheek had been snuggling against Hester's smooth blonde head and their bodies couldn't have been closer if they'd been grafted together, and Hester had looked transported. Ziggy could imagine why. It wasn't difficult. She too knew the magic of being held in Rafe's arms.

That had been the last she'd seen of him, and he was probably still with Hester, somewhere quiet, where they wouldn't be disturbed. And tonight might be the night when the blinkers finally fell from Rafe's eyes. The night when he recognised what Hester must have known all along—that they were right for each other. And he'd realise he'd been looking in the wrong direction when he'd misguidedly proposed to Ziggy. Hester would make a far more suitable future Lady Staineswick and mother of his sons.

Unaccountably, Ziggy felt sick. It must be the heat. It couldn't be the thought of Rafe being with Hester, because Ziggy herself had been the first to admit how well those two suited each other.

And when her partner reappeared with two laden plates, and Thurston, astonishingly solicitous—even smiling!—followed with a bottle of champagne on ice, procuring them a secluded table out of nowhere with the ease of a magician, Ziggy was unable to do more than pick at the food, which showed she was off colour because she normally ate like a horse.

Her eyes were beginning to glaze as her eager young escort began to re-tell the gory saga of his accident on the hunting field last season. She didn't know how she was going to listen to the story again without throwing up, and was trying to dream up an excuse for escaping when Rafe appeared, standing over them, dark, cool, handsome, with a quiet but friendly determination in his voice as he enquired, 'Good party, Clifford? Mind if I steal Ziggy for a moment? There's something we need to discuss.'

Relief intoxicated her, sending her sagging spirits soaring, and she didn't know whether it was because Rafe was here, seeking her out, or because the foxy-faced Clifford had withdrawn, no fuss at all, almost tugging his forelock.

She lifted her glass to him, slanting eyes sparkling over the rim as she waited for him to take Clifford's seat, but he said smoothly, not expecting an argument and for once not getting one, 'Bring that with you. We both need some air.'

There was air on the terrace, soft, sweet night air, and her movement, as she turned to him, was as natural as breathing.

He took the glass from her hand, putting it down on the stone balustrading, and her body quivered helplessly because she knew he was going to kiss her. Half of her wanted it, and half of her didn't. But she knew she wouldn't fight him. But he said, his mouth a tantalising breath away from hers, 'Do you do it consciously?'

'Do what?'

He puzzled her and she knew he had more than light dalliance on his mind. She trembled, torn between apprehension and wanting, her tongue flickering over her lips as he elucidated, 'Captivate. Bewitch. First Lord Staineswick and now myself.' His hands rested lightly at the base of her throat, the balls of his thumbs moving in a soft circle of weakening sensation, and this was only the beginning, and she raised her eyes to his, her lips parting in a mindless offering and he groaned, a husky, rended sound, adding, 'I don't give up on something

I've set my mind on. Remember that, my sweet, and don't come to me lightly.'

His voice carried a veiled warning. This was serious for him, and Ziggy took a pace backwards before his lips and hands and body could wreak their havoc, her arms hugging her body.

She knew he was referring to his proposal of marriage. She had refused him once, out of hand, not thinking too deeply about it because her mind had been confused, incapable of functioning properly, and she wondered now if her blind refusal had been right...

She carefully avoided the darkness of his eyes, set in features more harshly drawn in the icy wash of moonlight, and felt, suddenly, that she didn't know him.

Her ideas had been turned upside down and she had to get to know him again, as a person, not as a potential husband, or lover, and she wondered whether to tell him this, and whether he would understand if she did.

If she asked for time to get to know him properly—the real Rafe d'Anjou and not the lazy pleasure-seeker of her imaginings—would he agree? Or would he pursue her relentlessly, as he had said he would?

Before she could put it to the test, and before his hands could pull her quivering body to the hard length of his, Hester intruded, moving towards them over the paving like a pillar of dull red flame in her flounced silk dress.

'So there you both are! One does feel in need of a respite occasionally. Lovely party, though, Rafe. A huge success!'

The great house was silent, the last of the overnight guests having gone to bed an hour ago, and Ziggy walked slowly into the deserted ballroom, in darkness now except for the pale wash of moonlight that drifted in through the tall mullioned windows.

She felt oddly flat and drained, the spirit sucked out of her, but even though it was gone four in the morning she was unable to bring herself to go to bed, though her entire body ached with tiredness and her feet were on fire.

After Hester had intruded on the terrace Ziggy had gone back to the party, determined to play her part. These people had come to see her, to see how an ordinary Canadian girl would assume the aristocratic mantle of an earl's granddaughter, and she wasn't going to let Gramps down.

And so she had sparkled, circulated, danced and chattered, and even though her thoughts had continually homed in on Rafe, and what might have happened, been said, out there on the terrace had Hester not inflicted her presence, she had kept a smile on her face. She had seen him watching her performance from time to time, but he hadn't approached her again and she had danced many times, but never with him.

Moving listlessly across the deserted floor, her dark head bowed as though its weight were too much for her slender neck to bear, she stooped to retrieve a lily that had fallen from a massed bank of flowers and ferns, and cradled it gently in her hands.

The stately white bloom had been trampled by careless feet and her fingers idled softly over the crushed petals. All that remained of its former beauty was its scent, and she felt a kinship that brought a sigh to her lips.

'Why so sad?'

Her head lifted slowly, but her heart was quicker to pick up its beat as she met Rafe's eyes, deep silver in the moon-washed darkness. Out in the main hall, across the space between the open double doors of the ballroom, Thurston moved about his business, his footsteps slow,

like an old tired man. And Rafe turned from his intent
scrutiny of Ziggy's pale features and said firmly,

'Get along to bed, Thurston. I'll finish down here.
Has Mrs Thurston gone up?'

'Half an hour ago, sir.' The elderly man's feet shuffled
to a halt. 'I was just on my way to set the security system
for what's left of the night.'

'I'll see to that. Get to bed.' Warmth invaded Rafe's
voice. 'And thank you, Thurston. Everything went off
splendidly.'

Then they were alone in the empty ballroom, with the
scent of a thousand flowers lying on the still air. There
was not even the ghostly echo of music and laughter to
break the silence, and Ziggy shivered.

'Cold?' Rafe's deep voice was husky, and she shook
her head. She wasn't cold, but a goose had walked over
her grave and she had the oddest feeling that something
was ending. And his nearness made her soul shake.

He had removed the formal jacket of his evening suit
and his crisp white shirt was open at the neck, the untied
bow of his tie hanging rakishly, and his broad shoulders
seemed to offer a haven that Ziggy, in her strange *triste*
mood, needed to cling to—though she wasn't a girl who
clung.

Silently, he took the crushed bloom from her hands
and laid it gently on a table and he held out his arms to
her, as if he sensed her need, and she slipped into their
enfolding warmth as if she were going home.

His lips, as they found hers, were gentle, the smooth
soft pressure of his kiss exquisite. He made no move to
deepen the embrace, just held her gently because he knew
her mood. Mindlessly, her body melted into his, all
tiredness gone as she felt the kick of desire deep inside
her. Sensuously, her fingers searched for the nape of his

neck, revelled for a moment in the feel of crisp short hair against smooth warm skin, then splayed upwards, twining, touching the hardness of bone beneath the softness of his hair, and drawing his head down to hers because she suddenly needed more, much more, than gentle comfort.

But he resisted her unspoken plea and held her a little away from him, and she could have cried like a child because that was how she inexplicably felt. Young, lost and vulnerable, and she knew with a directness that startled her that she needed a friend, a loving friend, only one, and that one was Rafe.

He could be all things: friend, lover, confidant; and it had taken her this long to recognise it. He was strong, and right now she needed his strength as much as she needed his arms around her, his lips on hers.

But the tender interlude had not left him unscathed. She could feel the tension of that tautly held body, so close to the fragile, melting, moon-silvered length of hers. And the light of the moon was sufficient to show her the frantic beating of a pulse at the base of his exposed throat.

'You have to be exhausted.' His fingers tilted her face, the pads of his long fingers softly exploring the delicate hollows beneath her cheekbones, and her breath came out on a small ragged sigh as he lightly brushed her lips with his... 'Much as I'd like to take advantage of your lowered resistance—it's time for bed, for you, at least.' He raised his head, wry humour tugging at his mouth. 'No doubt you'll be back on form in the morning—your usual pert and impossible self. But if it's any comfort to you, Ziggy, my sweet, tonight you were everything anyone could wish you to be. Now——' he propelled her around and planted a gentle tap on her bottom, '—bed for you.'

Even if Ziggy had felt like a forlorn child a few moments ago, she didn't want to be treated like one, and she wriggled smartly round to face him again, her pointed chin characteristically high, colour stealing back to her cheeks as she blurted, 'If you think I'm impossible and pert, then why the heck did you ask me to marry you? And not too many weeks ago,' she went on scornfully, aghast at the devil inside her that was making her act this way, 'you said that the idea of tying yourself down didn't appeal. And you sounded as if you meant it!'

Her eyes had darkened now, were flashing, matching the sapphires at her throat, but inside she was crying because she knew she was erecting spiky defences between herself and the man who could have been her friend—and more, possibly very much more.

She shouldn't have mentioned that proposal, simply been content to take developments as they came, getting to know him better while she could. But Rafe didn't rise to her barbed remarks, merely commented lazily, 'A man can change his mind. It isn't entirely the female's exclusive right,' and he draped an arm around her shoulder, walking her to the double doors. 'You're too tired to fight, to think straight, even. And while, as I said before, I could take advantage of that, I won't. So, for the last time, Ziggy, goodnight!'

Which didn't exactly answer her question, and her fingernails dug into the palms of her hands as she repeated stubbornly, 'So what made you change your mind? Why should you want to marry me? All we ever do is fight!' That wasn't strictly true, but she was beyond thinking about the veracity of what she was saying, and she was incensed almost beyond control when he evaded her smoothly, walking away and leaving her at the foot of the staircase.

'Why do you think? It shouldn't be too difficult to work out.'

CHAPTER NINE

DESPITE not having crawled into bed until well after four, Ziggy was up before seven, too restless to sleep. Her encounter with Rafe in the deserted ballroom, as the rest of the house slept, had been frustratingly unsatisfactory. She had wanted to ask him to be her friend, to ask for time to get to know him, to consider his marriage proposal more deeply. She had wanted him to hold her, make love to her, but he had denied her everything, putting her away from him as if she were a tired child.

His enigmatic reply to her ill-timed question had been playing on her mind. But what, after all, had she expected him to say? That he was fathoms deep in love with her? Was that what she wanted?

Although it was early when she mooched downstairs there was plenty of activity. Thurston, no sign of fatigue on his impassive features now, was casting a critical eye over the table in the state dining room—not a lifeless set-piece now but laid to cater for the varying breakfasting needs of the house guests who would appear much later.

And his stiff, 'Good morning, miss. You'll find hot coffee in the kitchen,' was belied by the fatherly twinkle in his eyes, and Ziggy grinned at him because his brand of pompous pedantry, allied to his deep and abiding concern for the care of the Bellingham family, delighted her.

'I could do with gallons of the stuff,' she confessed. 'Last night was something else, but shattering!'

132

She wandered out of the room again, catching his dour, 'Quite so, Miss Ziggy,' and grinned again, calling goodmornings to those of the outdoor staff who were already at work dismantling the exotic floral decorations in the main hall.

Betty and Jane were in the huge kitchen, wrapping the remains of last night's feast in clingfilm, and Ziggy said, 'I hope you're going to take some of that lot home with you!'

Jane giggled, dealing with the salmon steaks. 'Madame d'Anjou said last night we was to take what we wanted. But my kids wouldn't know what had hit them if I put this on their plates. They'd sooner have fish fingers. But one of the sherry trifles wouldn't get the thumbs down! There's fresh coffee over there, miss.'

There was, plenty of it, and piping hot, and Mrs Thurston, pausing as she counted out rashers of bacon to be grilled later with kidneys for those with the stomach for a cooked breakfast, said, 'Help yourself, miss, do. I must say, you looked a picture last night. It did my heart good to see you, that's a fact.' Then, on an undertone, aware of sharp ears and stilled fingers among the clingfilm on the other side of the kitchen, 'And if one-who-shall-remain-nameless got her long nose out of joint, it isn't well before time! We all know where that one had set her sights—would have had to be blind as well as daft not to!—and not even she could have been so thick-skinned as to miss how Mr Rafe only had eyes for you.'

All of which left Ziggy gawping, not understanding any of it until, two cups of strong coffee later, swallowed while leaning against one of the vast stainless steel sinks, her wits lost a few woolly edges.

The housekeeper had obviously been talking about Hester. Mixing freely with the staff as Ziggy did, helping out on occasion, she had first-hand knowledge of the way Hester Povey was viewed. She was a good guide, treating the tourists who came to see over the house more as valued guests than paying trippers. And her attitude to the Earl was pleasantly respectful, her manner without fault. But on the other side of the green baize door, so to speak, her pretty manners deserted her completely.

And Mrs Thurston hadn't failed to notice how Hester's eyes followed Rafe with doglike devotion, and she and the rest of the staff were probably dreading the day when Rafe began to show signs of real reciprocation. No one would want to work under Hester as the future Earl's wife.

Ziggy washed her cup at the sink and hung it with its mates on a hook on one of the immense dressers. It would make Mrs Thurston's day if she were to confide that Rafe had asked the Colonial last of the line to be his wife—not the Colonel's so-suitable daughter!

But she wouldn't do that, of course, because marrying anyone, especially the one man she'd met who seemed able to master her—body, soul and mind—so effortlessly, wasn't something Ziggy felt remotely ready for.

She enjoyed her independence, the feeling of being in charge of herself and her future, far too much for the total commitment a man like Rafe would demand—and get!

If she ever married it would be to a man who took her as she was, warts and all, a man she loved, felt at ease with, a man who made very few demands. Not a man like Rafe who never failed to point out her faults, with whom she never felt entirely easy. Who could feel

easy when tension was always there, when she was either
boiling with rage or melting with a physical need that
made her feel she had no control over her body? Before
meeting him she had never been the type of girl to allow
her instincts to overrule her common sense.

Outside it was misty, a sign of another fine day to
come, and Ziggy, her hands thrust in the torn pockets
of her oldest, shabbiest jeans—which were the first things
she'd laid her hands on this morning—struck out in the
direction of the Butterfly House.

Over the past few weeks, while Rafe had been away,
she had often been drawn there, sometimes working
behind the counter in the gift shop or restaurant if they'd
been short-staffed. The place had never lost its appeal
and this morning, after the Midsummer Ball—to which
all the staff had been invited—she might be needed to
help out.

But part-way over the meadow she paused. It was only
just gone eight, and no one would have arrived yet to
open up. So she struck out at a tangent, killing time,
following a ghost of a track, almost lost in the long grass,
leading to trees that had surrendered their verdant
greenness to the shimmering grey mist.

Her thoughts, as they always did when she was not
fully occupied, turned to Rafe, and she worried away at
his remark, 'Why do you think? It shouldn't be too difficult to work out.' The simplest reason she could come
up with was unbelievable, and she turned it over in a
mind that was growing more astonished by the second.
Why did a man propose to a girl? Answer: because the
man in question loved the girl.

But that didn't seem credible. Rafe, in love with her?
Hardly likely! Or was it? She didn't know, and she felt
fluttery and strange. He had stopped regarding her as a

greedy tramp, she knew that. And he did fancy her. She wasn't very experienced, but she was bright enough to know when a man was aroused! But men could get aroused by women they didn't love, didn't even like!

It was all such a muddle, like a maze with no way out! Only last night he'd called her pert and impossible, so he couldn't possibly love her, could he?

But despite the denial of her brain her knees went weak at the very thought of his being in love with her, and they threatened to collapse completely when Rafe appeared in front of her, emerging through the mists like an uncanny materialisation of her thoughts.

Something closely akin to physical pain stabbed a burning track clear through her as she recognised the figure at his side. Hester. The pain deepened, spiralling sharply inside her, making her eyes go dark, and she couldn't have answered his easy 'Hi, there!' if her entire future had depended on it.

Hester was looking chipper and businesslike in a pleated fawn skirt, a matching jacket slung casually over her shoulders, giving a glimpse of a dark sage blouse. She looked as though she'd enjoyed a full eight hours' sleep, but she couldn't have done, because she'd been one of the last to leave last night.

Conscious of the dark rings round her own eyes, of her oldest clothes pulled on all anyhow, Ziggy did her best not to scowl at Hester. Which was difficult, especially when that lady, all sparkly eyes and prettily smiling lips, announced, 'I'm just on my way to do something about those cut flowers. Leave them to the Thurstons, or the rest of the staff, and they'd be gracing someone else's sideboard tonight!'

'Oh, really!' Ziggy's nostrils flared. She, who had been at Staineswick for such a relatively short time, knew full

well that none of the staff would take so much as a crumb
without permission, and Hester should have known that
too. Maybe she'd been born with a nasty suspicious
mind, the sort that thought the inferior 'peasants' would
slit her throat as soon as look at her. And she hated
Hester for that insensitive, denigrating remark.

And for something else too, she realised as the import
of the pain she felt finally reached her brain. If Hester
was on her way to Staineswick from her home, as Ziggy
knew she was, taking the short cut over the meadow,
then what was Rafe doing at her side? Early-morning
escort duty in case the fragile little lady got attacked by
muggers or a passing pack of wolves!

Ziggy didn't think so. She didn't like what she *did*
think, either. Last night she had longed for Rafe to hold
her, and the mood she'd been in would have made her
a pushover if he had been inclined to take things as far
as she would permit. But he had said he wouldn't take
advantage of her lowered resistance. Why? Because he
was too much of a gentleman? Or because he was on
his way to Hester's bed?

In the light of present circumstances the latter seemed
far more likely! And for some incomprehensible reason
Ziggy wanted to curl up in a hole and die. Just die!

So when Rafe, having watched the brief interchange
between the two girls in amused silence, asked patron-
isingly, 'And where do you think you're going, so early
in the morning? I expected you to be still catching up
on your beauty sleep!' she could have hit him, and damn
near did!

Only Hester's superior cat-who-has-eaten-the-canary
smirk stopped her. And as Hester, who could have gone
to bed little earlier than Ziggy had—and who had been
occupied with something other than sleep when she'd

got there, if the dark suspicions she was harbouring were correct—could look new-penny fresh, then the clear implication was that Ziggy looked grotty, in need of another ten hours' shut-eye at least, and couldn't stand the pace!

Scowling darkly at that lean annoying face, she snapped rudely, 'Minding my own business!' then regretted it as she saw the way his eyes narrowed to icily glittering slits, denoting, as she knew from past and vivid experience, that she was infuriating him.

But at least there was little he could do or say to relieve his rage, not with the simpering Hester attached to his side like a well-bred limpet, and that was a comfort. And he had said she'd be back to being her usual pert and impossible self this morning, so who was she to prove him wrong?

So when he took her arm in a hand that was far from gentle, and said in a voice that was controlled enough not to be *quite* a growl, 'You'd better get back to the house. And change out of those wretched jeans. Your grandfather's guests will be coming down for breakfast by now, and we wouldn't want to deny them the pleasure of taking their leave of you, would we?' she took great pleasure in digging her heels in and refusing to budge an inch.

He was a sarcastic brute! Treating her like a disagreeable child in the past had been one thing. It had been just between the two of them. But now the perfect Hester was listening, and lapping it up. Hester was always beautifully groomed, and it wouldn't have entered Hester's noble little head to neglect her duty and run out on house guests.

Truth to tell, Ziggy hadn't given the overnighters a thought, except to surmise that those who actually did manage to crawl out of bed before noon would be so hung over that all they'd want to do was slink away, drawing the least possible attention to themselves!

But she wasn't going to make excuses, or try her brand of humour on him to see if it matched his. She knew it would, and right now she needed to stay angry with him.

'I'm sure they'll make do with your smiling little face!' she glowered up into that dark and definitely unsmiling visage and wrenched her arm free, tugging petulantly at the collar of her admittedly disreputable shirt. 'I'm off to the Butterfly House, and some civilised company.'

She began to lope away, her long legs carrying her over the meadow at a pace Hester's much shorter ones wouldn't be able to cope with—and Rafe would stay at that little lady's side, wouldn't he? He wouldn't leave her to make her own way through the mist, would he? Not when he'd obviously spent what had been left of last night in her bed, he wouldn't!

A few yards on, she turned, seeing the two of them standing together. A well-matched couple, she thought sourly. Rafe's face was murderous, she expected that, and Hester's was gloating, and she'd expected that too. But she hadn't been expecting the resurge of pain, the sheer shrivelling pain. So she called out, her voice honey strongly laced with vinegar, 'Better get a move on, hadn't you? Before the staff nick the silver along with the left-over flowers!'

Ziggy sat on a bench inside the Butterfly House, perspiring gently. It was strange to think that these colourful, glorious creatures emerged from dull and uninteresting chrysalises. But it happened, a sort of miracle.

She heaved a shaky sigh as a Painted Lady, a perfect specimen, settled on her knee, and held her breath until it fluttered away again. Yes, the miracle happened and there was a parallel in her own life. Only, on the whole, it was really more like a disaster than a miracle, because she'd been happy the way she was.

Her mind and her heart had emerged from the strait-jacket of her own view of others—and of herself. They had been emerging for weeks and she hadn't fully acknowledged it.

Her preconceived notions of Gramps' character, and Rafe's, had undergone a sea change. And on the physical side she had seen the transformation that good clothes, carefully chosen, could make. So the gawky, spiky chrysalis had been made over and had ended up as a butterfly, and had actually enjoyed the process!

But worse than that, far worse, was the newly acquired knowledge that she loved Rafe. Was hopelessly in love with him. Wanted him, now and for ever. And that, with the attendant implications, put the very last vestige of her old self in jeopardy.

Ziggy Bellingham, free and independent spirit, could so easily be hogtied to a man whose least touch, lightest word, would have her melting, mindless and meek.

And she didn't at all know whether she could stand living the rest of her life with a meek and mindless self!

'Are you trying to get heatstroke in here?' Mike's amused voice came from somewhere behind her shoulder, and she carefully plastered a smile on her face before turning.

'I thought the Turkish bath effect might help, after last night!'

'I know what you mean.' He made a sympathetic noise in his throat and sat down beside her. 'The wine flowed a little too freely for my feeble willpower. But it was a great party.'

They'd had a few dances together—the giggly, Top-of-the-Pops type because Mike had downed a few glasses too many and had been inclined to get amorous in the slower, smoochier numbers. Now Ziggy sighed, wishing she could put the clock back, wishing she hadn't walked in the meadow this morning because then she wouldn't have seen Rafe with Hester, and what the eye didn't see...

Hearing the sigh, taking it to portend a headache on a par with his own, Mike said bracingly, 'You looked great last night. Like a fairy-tale come true,' and Ziggy countered quickly, because over the weeks she had got to know him well, liked what she knew, but didn't want him to get ideas that couldn't be put into action,

'I'm afraid this particular fairy-tale has a heroine who feels like a jaundiced frog this morning!' Then she stood up, wondering if Rafe had really been with Hester last night or whether their being together had been a co-incidence, and determining to ask him if he ever calmed down enough for her to bring the subject up.

'I'm going to get a cold drink,' she explained, unsurprised when Mike stood up too.

'I'll join you. They say orange juice is good for hangovers. Vitamin C, or something.'

They took their chilled juice outside, to a table in the shade, and Pam, who served behind the counter in the restaurant, called out, 'Fabulous do last night! Why can't you go away and get found again!' and Ziggy dredged up a smile, agreeing that yes, it had been fun, and wishing that everything was as straightforward as that.

But Mike, with keener eyes, asked, 'What's up, love?' and Ziggy shrugged, twisting the cool glass between her fingers as he took the seat opposite hers.

Doubtfully she glanced up at him, then smiled. He wasn't a gossip and she knew his friendship would extend

to a sympathetic ear, and it might be good to unburden
herself—if only partly.

'I guess I'm unsettled.' And that was something she
might have been able to say to Rafe, but she could never
tell Gramps. The last thing she wanted to do was hurt
him, and he thought she had settled perfectly at
Staineswick. As, in a way, she had. 'You talked about
a fairy-tale come true. Well, Staineswick's like that, for
me. I love it, but I feel threatened.'

'How come?' Mike's eyes were puzzled. 'You've got
it made. Oh, I don't mean money-wise, nothing as crass
as that,' he disclaimed. 'But your grandfather openly
dotes on you, you have a home anyone in their right
mind would envy—for as long as you want it——' his
voice tailed off on a verbal shrug and Ziggy knew he
was right.

She was lucky, perhaps too lucky. She was becoming
too deeply involved with it all. With Staineswick,
Gramps, Rafe... She felt unsure of herself for the first
time in her life.

Part of her wanted to leave, to pick up her life while
she still had a slight chance, and part of her wanted to
stay, to allow this new and shattering love for Rafe to
grow. To forget, if she could, that he might have been
with Hester last night...

'I feel as if the future's pressing in on me, uncertain
and misty. I feel——' But how could she explain how
she felt—about Rafe, about Hester—when her own mind
was too muddled to understand? 'I feel—peculiar, keyed
up and tense,' she offered hopelessly, and Mike laughed,
laying a hand over hers.

'That's called a hangover! But seriously,' his fingers
curled round hers and she allowed her hand to lie pass-
ively trapped beneath his because it was comforting to

know someone cared enough to try to soothe her, 'I can understand how you must feel. You were just an ordinary girl with the sort of life-style millions of other girls share, and you found yourself here, heir to a fortune, with a titled grandfather who loves you—and because he loves you, expects a great deal from you. And sometimes you get the blues, like now, and you hanker after the old life when nothing more pressing than what to eat for dinner or whether you could afford a new pair of jeans *and* pay the rent cropped up! Am I right?'

'I guess you must be.' He was too, but his hypothesis begged the question of Rafe, of her reaction to him, of his to her, of their future—if they could make one together. And that was a very vexed question indeed.

Ziggy suddenly felt tearful, so she smiled at Mike to divert the flood, and she tried to look carefree, as if he had taken a load off her mind, and he lifted her hand to his mouth and kissed it—as Rafe's voice came from two feet away, sounding like breaking ice.

'I thought I'd find you still here. Your grandfather has been asking for you.'

'And what was that all about?' he asked, tight-lipped, crashing gears as if wrecking the Range Rover was something he dearly wanted to do as they bounced and jolted over the meadow.

His face was grim as he went on witheringly, 'How often do you and Mike play out tender little love scenes in full view of every passing visitor—not to mention the rest of the staff?'

Ziggy sniffed. She didn't know why she loved this oaf! Quite possibly, she was deranged. She jerked her nose in the air and replied with justifiable tartness, 'What's wrong? Isn't it the done thing for an earl's grand-daughter to hobnob with one of the *hoi polloi*?'

'You know damn well that's not what I mean!' thundered Rafe, and Ziggy enquired, acid-sweet,

'Then what do you advocate? That I follow your example and play out my love scenes in private, in the early hours, with someone perfect enough never to kiss and tell?'

'And what the hell is that supposed to mean?'

They were off the meadow, on to the drive, and he went even faster now, and if they'd had a longer runway they might just have got airborne. But Ziggy wasn't going to give him a hint that when he was mad with her his driving terrified her, or that her own feelings for him, so newly discovered, were terrifying her even more.

She hadn't wanted to fall in love, not for years yet, and then, most certainly, not with an arrogant, domineering, do-as-you're-damned-well-told type like this!

But love moves mysteriously, she thought gloomily, and wondered if she'd loved him all along, since the day he'd watched her in Covent Garden. Most likely, she was daft enough!

She risked a sideways glance at his forbidding profile. He surely was mad as hell at her! For skipping her duties back at the house, or for allowing Mike to kiss her hand? And the thought occurred that maybe, just maybe, the guy was jealous! And if he was going through anything like the agony she'd experienced this morning, when bumping into him and Hester, and her dreadful jealousy had finally opened her eyes to the fact that she loved him, then he must be suffering hell!

That should have made her feel sympathetic, but it didn't. It made her feel squirmy inside, and happy. So very happy!

When he wasn't quite so cross, she'd ask him about Hester. Ask him if he loved her, and if he said yes she'd consider his proposal. Because she might find, all things being equal, that she could come to terms with being tied to this man for ever, after all...

CHAPTER TEN

THE RANGE ROVER roared to a halt in the stable yard and Rafe leaned over her, flinging open the door at her side.

'Might as well get out here.' His words were clipped and expressionless and he didn't look at her. He had been so close, leaning over her, and his closeness had taken her breath away, tightened her throat.

But now he was back squarely in his own seat, his fingers drumming against the steering wheel, impatient to be rid of her. A lump rose in Ziggy's throat, threatening to choke her. She wanted to touch the warm skin of that tanned forearm—only inches away—to run her fingers over that whipcord-covered thigh, to press herself into his arms and seek the mind-blowing sensation of his kiss. To hear him say he'd make everything all right, that he loved her...

And couldn't the brute see the change in her? Didn't he know she loved him? The tardy realisation of that love had hit Ziggy right between the eyes and it must have left a mark for everyone to see! Something had ended for her last night, after the Ball. She had sensed it and it had turned her cold, and she knew, at last, what it was. Her footloose, uncommitted life had gone for good. She was no longer her own woman, she was Rafe's.

'Taken root to the seat?' He sounded as if he hated her, and it hurt. Her face tightened with misery and she swung her long legs sideways, scrambling out before he could see the glitter of shaming tears. Not that he was looking her way. He was staring straight ahead, grim-faced, and she didn't acknowledge his terse, 'I'll see you later. We have things to talk out', because it sounded more like a threat than anything else, and there was no answer to that.

She stood on the cobbles, the hot sun burning down, watching as he ran the vehicle into one of the converted stables. It was no use wishing she didn't love him, because she did. She wanted to cry. And suddenly, with an intensity that made her flesh shake, she was consumed by jealousy.

Sudden and shatteringly realistic mind pictures of what might have happened in the early morning hours of this morning before Rafe had walked back to Staineswick with Hester made her stomach curl with agony, and she walked unsteadily over the yard to the door which led to the vast kitchen regions, knowing that Rafe had been right. They had to talk. Their relationship had to move beyond this present wariness. She couldn't bear the uncertainty.

He had asked her to marry him, but she didn't know why. He could be tender, passionate, warm—all these things. But he also treated her like a disagreeable child and the only times when he made his emotions clear—with words—were when he was shredding her with his tongue!

And what place, if any, did Hester have in his life? If he and Hester had been lovers Ziggy could stand that—just. Provided the affair was killed stone-dead. Now.

Betty was preparing a coffee tray in the kitchen, and Ziggy pulled herself together and asked, 'Is that for Gramps?'

'No, love, it's for Madame d'Anjou. She's in the small drawing-room.'

Betty was fortyish, built like a bolster, and she usually looked as if she hadn't a care in the world. But today she looked harassed; the last few days had been a hectic time for everyone, and Ziggy said, 'I'll take it through. Why don't you have a cup yourself and put your feet up for ten minutes?'

Léonie was writing letters at a small escritoire in one of the window bays, and she didn't look up when Ziggy pushed the door open with her foot.

'Oh, thank you, Betty. Just put the tray down anywhere.'

'It's me,' Ziggy said. 'Rafe said Gramps wanted to see me?'

Léonie laid aside the sheet of paper, smiling as she turned.

'He did. But I don't think it was that important. He's out somewhere with Arnold now, but he'll be back for lunch. You're joining me for coffee? Good.' She rose stiffly to her feet. 'This morning I am feeling my age! But it was a wonderful party and you were a great success. Your grandfather's very proud of you.'

That was good to hear, but somewhere, amid the turmoil of her emotions, guilt pricked at Ziggy's conscience as she took her coffee and joined Léonie on a small plushy sofa.

'Did everyone get away this morning? I guess I should have been here to say goodbye and thank you for coming.'

'Nonsense!' Léonie liked her coffee strong and black and she sipped the hot brew with relish. 'Ah, that's better! Much better! Now, where were we? Ah yes—yes, we got the overnight people away earlier than we'd thought and as you weren't around—everyone thought you were still sleeping and wouldn't hear of your being disturbed—they were all free to say how lovely you were, and how happy Lord Staineswick must be to have you at home after all these years. Something, being English, with those carefully cultivated stiff upper lips, they wouldn't have felt comfortable saying to your face!'

The older woman produced an enamelled case from a pocket in her billowing peacock blue robe and extracted one of the thin black cigarettes she used, lighting it and blowing a plume of blue smoke to the ornately plastered and decorated ceiling.

'I'm beginning to feel human at last! So tell me,' she tapped Ziggy's jeans-clad knee, 'where have you been?'

'Playing truant,' Ziggy confessed wryly, fiddling restlessly with the single heavy braid of hair that fell over her shoulder, almost reaching her lap. 'I got up at seven and ended up at the Butterfly House.'

'My God!' Léonie rolled brown eyes to the ceiling. 'The stamina you young people have! That son of mine brought a pot of tea to my room just before seven—waking me from a perfectly good sleep just because he hadn't been able to sleep himself! He was going to get dressed, he said. And go out for a walk, he said. He had something on his mind—some problem he had to work out how best to tackle—he said! He didn't even tell me what the problem was; that *might* have made up for being woken at such an uncivilised hour! Children!' she groaned. 'They never cease to be a trouble and worry, no matter how old they get to be! But I do believe,' she gave Ziggy a knowing smile, 'with a mother's instincts for these things, that the "problem" on his mind was you. You stunned that cool customer of a son of mine last night. Positively poleaxed him! When he wasn't involved in a duty dance he was lounging around, looking

mean, moody and magnificent, his eyes glued on you!'
she ended with wicked, unmaternal glee.

And Ziggy, trying to keep her voice dry, drawled, 'That
I can just see!'

But inside her heart was doing somersaults, crazy twists
and leaps of unadulterated joy. So Rafe hadn't spent the
early hours with Hester. He too had been unable to
sleep—the evidence of his mother's words, the pot of
early tea, proved that. He, like her, had risen early,
walked outside in the mist. And he'd met up with Hester,
dutiful Hester on her way to the big house to sort out
the flowers, and had simply been making his way back
with her when Ziggy had seen them and leapt to all the
wrong conclusions!

She felt as if a huge black cloud had lifted from her.
Free as air, and happy... happy!

Thurston had told her that Rafe was busy in his office,
had asked for a sandwich and coffee to be taken to him
at lunchtime because he didn't want to be disturbed to
eat with the family.

Well, Ziggy was going to disturb him. And how!

It didn't take long to change out of her tatty jeans
and shirt and slip into a cool cotton sleeveless shift that
matched the colour of her eyes. She cinched the narrow
belt around the neat span of her waist and stepped into
high-heeled mules. Then, on impulse, she unbraided her
hair and brushed it until it hung, straight as a jetty
waterfall, down her back. A spray of Joy, the lightest
touch of scarlet on her lips, and she was ready.

Ready to apologise for the way she'd been this
morning. To ask how he felt about her, really felt, and
confess her own love for him. And then—well, the future
would be up to him because her future, without him,
would be no future at all.

The flutters of excitement inside her made her legs feel like jelly as she hurried down the stairs. But if her shaking knees gave way, and she fell, it wouldn't matter because she could fly the rest of the way down! Her feet had grown wings, hadn't they?

Rafe looked like a man with a lot on his mind, and Ziggy's heart blossomed with love. He had had a bad night and the day hadn't got any better. He lifted stony eyes from his paperwork as she closed the door softly behind her and stood looking at him, her eyes misty.

How she loved this man! Loved every inch of that lean hard body, every plane and angle of that handsome, unsmiling face, the dark ravaged eyes above the decisive cut of high cheekbones. Loved every facet of his quick, incisive mind.

'Well?' His mouth indented sourly. He looked as if he'd been through a bad time, and she was the one who'd put him through it.

After those brief, tender moments they'd shared last night he wouldn't have been able to believe his senses when the melting, willing woman in his arms had changed, overnight, into a spiteful-tongued child. And she was sorry. So sorry——

She said, very quickly because she had to get it out of the way, 'I want to apologise for the way I was this morning. I thought you and Hester had just got out of her bed.'

It took some seconds for her words to sink in, and when they did his face was a mask of fury. 'My God! What is this?' He flung his pen away from him, sending it clattering over the desk, and pushed himself to his feet, his eyes raking over her, spilling contempt wherever they touched—from her anxious face right down to her long, slender legs, the elegant feet in the high-heeled shoes.

His mouth tightened perceptibly and he bunched his hands in the pockets of his narrow-fitting trousers and turned his back on her, his anger explicit in the way the wide shoulder muscles tensed, in the bitter ice of his words.

'I ask you to spend your life with me, as my wife. Offer to share everything I have with you. Commit my future to you. And you can believe that of me? That I'd hold you in my arms last night, then creep away to some furtive assignation with another woman! I thought I knew you at last, believed I'd reached behind the prickly exterior and found the true woman—beautiful, warm, capable of love. My God!' he hurled himself round, his blazing scornful eyes searing her soul, 'I don't know you at all!'

Her own eyes flickered beneath the assault of his and she shook her head slowly, negating the meaning behind his tortured words. Put like that, it did sound bad. But when she'd seen him with Hester and jumped to the wrong conclusions, she hadn't known she loved him. She had, of course, but she simply hadn't had the wits to acknowledge it. It had taken the pain of jealousy to open her eyes, and up until then she had been too busy erecting barriers as soon as he had broken them down.

'I've said I'm sorry, and I mean it.' All at once Ziggy felt older, wiser, in control. She went towards him, not hurrying, because there was all the time in the world to get it right. 'I was blinded by jealousy. You can understand that?'

Thick dark lashes, tipped with gold, briefly veiled his eyes, and when they met hers again there was a question there, and she smiled. Of course he understood. His caustic remarks regarding Mike this morning could only have stemmed from jealousy.

She went to him, sinuous and slow, and when their bodies were just touching she gently placed her hands on his chest, feeling the vital warmth of him, the heavy beat of his heart beneath her palms.

She was making love to him with every breath she took, and surely he must know that, it wasn't hard. It was the easiest thing in the world.

Her eyes left his and dropped to linger on his mouth, on the hard incisive twist that didn't fool her because she had felt the way his body stiffened, the increased beat of his heart, the sudden thrust of his loins against the softness of her belly. Her own desire unfurled, her femininity responding to his potent masculinity, and as his arms at last came round her, crushing her close to the length of him, she knew that loving this man was the most devastating emotion she would ever feel.

Blindly, she raised her face to his, drinking in its savage male beauty, and she whispered throatily, 'Do you love me?' and he came back roughly,

'Right now I think I loathe you!' and took her lips with a passion that made nonsense of his words and sent the two of them, clinging together as if they were one entity, hurtling into orbit.

Rafe was groaning softly, kissing her as if he couldn't get enough of her, her eyes, her lips, her throat; his hands ranging her body, turning her to fire, and as her mouth found the pulse at the base of his throat he breathed raggedly,

'God, I want you! You're driving me out of my mind!'

Ziggy pulled in a shuddering breath. In a few more moments they would be making love right here on the office floor, and she wanted more than that for them.

The first time had to be perfect. And she wondered if it was already too late as his fingers dealt with the buttons on her dress, exposing rounded inviting breasts...

But she tried, gallantly, half hoping her reasoning wouldn't work, that he would take her here and now, because if her words couldn't stop him, she knew she couldn't...

'I think we should call a halt here,' she muttered breathlessly, and Rafe's fingers stilled as his smoky eyes locked with hers. The depth of his desire was written plainly and his lips moved slowly, as if he were having trouble getting himself together.

'You'll marry me?'

'Yes. I love you.' He held her, close, but without the driving passion of a few moments ago, one strong hand on her back, the other cradling her head against the width of his shoulders, his fingers splayed in the midnight darkness of her hair, and Ziggy knew that this was the most perfect moment in her life. She was his woman, now and for always.

His mouth nuzzled her ear and his voice was thick. 'We'll make beautiful children together. An heir for Staineswick, another for Saint-Valéry-en-Caux——' and she snorted, cutting him off.

'And what if they're all girls? What price your heirs then? After six baby females I'll give up trying to give you males. So take warning!' She smiled, feeling his teeth nip her earlobe, because even in the first throes of the total and shattering realisation of love she had found a snappy comeback. Meek and mindless? Oh no, she'd never be that!

She would love him until the end of her days, but she would never be hogtied. The essential spirit of Ziggy Bellingham was not in jeopardy, as she had feared it might be. Loving this man, being loved by him, could only enrich her, give her life a new and deeper dimension.

She felt his answering grin, heard his amused, 'Only six? Give up easily, don't you!' then he held her away from him, just a little, his hands gentle, his eyes warming her. His mouth brushed hers softly and she went weak with her need of him, her love for him. But he smiled crookedly, moving away from her and raking his fingers through his hair.

'You were absolutely right. We have to call a halt to this.' But there was deep regret in his eyes, mirroring her own, and he rumpled her hair. 'I've got a mass of paperwork to get through. Once it's done I'll be able to devote all my time to you. And Ziggy——' he was already standing behind the desk, one hand resting on a thick box file, 'can you keep our news until dinner this evening? I want to be with you when we break it to Dudley and Léonie. I can't wait to see their faces!' His eyes were alight with warmth and laughter and love for her and she said,

'Yes, of course, we must tell them together.'

'And after, we'll find a quiet place, just the two of us, and we'll talk about details. Like how soon we can be married—it's going to have to be a splashy affair, you won't mind?'

Ziggy shook her head, nothing mattered but the fact that they were to be married, and Rafe offered a sop of comfort.

'Not the actual ceremony, of course, the Bellingham private chapel won't accommodate too many, but the reception could make last night look like a small family tea-party. And there'll be reporters from the expensive glossies, not to mention those from the daily dreadfuls, because that sort of thing is expected when the heir and heiress to a great estate tie the knot. But I promise you the honeymoon will be quiet!'

Ziggy nodded, her heart hammering too quickly to allow coherent speech because his eyes were telling her that later this evening, alone, they would have more to occupy them than the discussion of wedding dates and protocol. But she managed, at last,

'Can I help here?' and he grinned.

'No way. If you stayed here I'd get no work done at all.' Then, considering her, he said, 'Why don't you take a nap after lunch? Catch up on last night's lost sleep. Dream of me—and you can tell me, later, if the reality matches imagination!'

The arrival of his lunch tray saved Ziggy the embarrassment of any comments he might have made regarding the flush of vivid colour his words had brought to her cheeks, and she made her escape, not really wanting to go at all because she wanted to be where he was. Always.

Her complete lack of appetite at lunch time was explained away by a fictitious surfeit of food and drink the night before. She was far too excited to eat. All she wanted to do was go to her room, maybe take that nap Rafe had mentioned, and dream of him. Or simply lie on her bed, allowing the fantastic reality of her love for him, and his for her, to sink in. It still seemed like a dream, only the fact that she was still trembling inside from the effects of being held in his arms reminded her that the events of the morning were not a product of wishful thinking.

But she wasn't allowed the luxury of sloping away, of letting her mind concentrate on the wonder of loving Rafe, because when Léonie rose from the table, Gramps said, 'I'd like a word with you, Ziggy.'

Léonie smiled. 'I'll leave you to it.'

So that quiet time with her thoughts of the man who was going to be her husband was surrendered. Gramps had wanted to talk to her this morning, she recalled, but Léonie had said she didn't think it was important, so it shouldn't take long.

'I've been meaning to ask you if you'd like to invite your mother over for a visit. I'd like to get to know the woman my son married. Do you think she'd come?'

'Like a shot!' Ziggy laughed. Only once she was here she would probably never go away! In her letters she'd sounded over the moon because of who her father-in-law was, and she'd probably been dining out on the story for weeks.

'Good. Make whatever arrangements suit you both.' And then, at a tangent, 'You looked beautiful last night. And I think the future Lord Staineswick was suitably impressed.'

Somehow, lately, she had forgotten to think of Rafe as the future Earl, and although she was still smiling a small frown appeared between her eyes as the present Earl leaned forward, his hands clasped loosely on the snowy linen table covering, his eyes twinkling.

'I must confess I was beginning to fear he'd never stop looking on you as an aggravating child!'

'Gramps?' Her frown deepened. 'What are you trying to say?' But a smile still hovered at the corners of her mouth. If only he knew how Rafe really saw her! As his lover, his wife, the mother of his children...

But he replied to her question with one of his own.

'And what are your feelings for Rafe?' then he grinned broadly as colour washed over her face. 'You don't need to answer that, my dear! When he came back to Staineswick last night I saw you come alive!'

He ignored her confusion, for which she was grateful. It was a bit humiliating, really, to know that Gramps—and who knew who else—had recognised the way she felt about Rafe before she had realised it herself!

'I can come clean now,' he chuckled. 'I've been watching and hoping for such a sign since the moment you arrived here. Being a wily old bird, however, I didn't mention my hopes until I was sure of my ground!'

'Hopes?' Ziggy stared at him, her slanting eyes clouding as unease began to make itself felt. And it deepened as he smiled back at her,

'Yes. Big ones. That you might grow to feel enough for Rafe to consider marriage?' A shaggy white brow lifted questioningly. 'I've known him since he was a child, and I admire what I know. And since tragic circumstances made him my heir I've felt more than confident about leaving Staineswick in his hands. And that confidence extends to you—the most precious possession of all. When I first saw you, got to know you, I knew that nothing could be better than a match between you and Rafe. Staineswick would become your home—you fit in here, you were meant to be here—and the estate would be kept together. And my grandchild would, in the fullness of time, inherit. You must see how perfect that would be.' Then, as if sensing the disquiet that hurried through her, taking possession, he assured her, 'But only if it would make you happy—that has to be the most important factor of all. And I have a sneaking suspicion that it would. I'm old, but not too old to remember how a woman's eyes glow when she looks at the man she loves!'

Afterwards, Ziggy was unable to remember how she got herself out of the room, how she had replied to that astute old matchmaker—or even if she had replied at all.

She had reached the top of the stairs before she realised where she was and wondered what she was doing, where she was going. And at first she scarcely noticed Hester, walking along the gallery towards her, until she said, 'Oh, Ziggy, I've put the last of the roses from last night in your room—and I think I may as well call it a day now.'

'Yes, of course.' Ziggy answered automatically, her mind on another plane. Something was worrying her and she didn't want to put a name to it.

She watched Hester walk down the staircase, her movements neat and graceful as always, and she thought, she acts as if she owns this place, then shrugged the grumbling thought aside. If Gramps was happy to allow Hester to make herself useful, to make herself at home, it should be no concern of hers.

Silently she wandered along the gallery, gravitating instinctively to the portrait of her grandmother. Apart from the clothes they wore, they could have been twins. Had Gramps started to think in terms of a marriage between herself and Rafe because he wanted to see the girl who looked so like the woman he'd loved installed as undisputed mistress here? The mother of the child who would one day inherit, flesh of his flesh, blood of his blood? Had the undoubted benefits of a match between his granddaughter, the last of the direct line, and the much admired man who was now his heir, followed on that initial reaction?

And had Rafe known of his wishes in that direction? The question that had been worrying her was out in the open and now she couldn't ignore it. If Gramps had kept his hopes to himself, until today, after he had recognised for himself how she felt about Rafe, then there was not a single thing to worry about.

But if he had spoken, much earlier, to Rafe on the subject... Ziggy hardly dared face the implications of that, and she stared into the painted blue eyes as if she could find the answer there.

Gramps and Rafe were very close, had been for years, and Rafe was astute enough to understand the financial advantages of such a marriage. The estate would be kept as an entity, not divided between two branches of the family. Such a division would be the last thing Rafe would want to see—not for his personal sake, but for Staineswick's. So had Gramps mentioned his hopes, and had Rafe decided to gratify them?

She went cold at the thought, and hugged her arms around her body, remembering how astonished she'd been when he'd proposed that night in London. Up until then all they'd ever done was fight! And she hadn't been able to understand exactly what had happened to make him decide he wanted her permanently in his life when not long before he'd as good as told her to get out of it!

He had been aware of her sexually, that had become very apparent by then, and he'd known that he could get her to respond to him on a physical level. Had he regarded that as a bonus, the incentive to opt for an expedient marriage? Something to make such a marriage just about tolerable?

She recalled with a clarity that made her feel ill that he had never said he loved her. Had the words stuck in his throat because they were untrue? And when she'd asked him, a few short hours ago, he'd replied that he loathed her! Had that been the truth?

Horrified by the paths her thoughts were dragging her along, Ziggy ran back down the stairs. A few hours ago she had promised to marry Rafe, and yet here she was, harbouring all kinds of sneaky disloyal thoughts. She ought to have her head examined for doubting him for one moment!

All she had to do was ask him if her grandfather had ever mentioned the subject of their possible marriage, spelled out the undeniable advantages it would bring. And if he said no, she would believe it, because she could trust him with her life.

Feeling considerably happier, she paused as she approached the door to his office, getting herself together. She mustn't allow him to guess how she'd doubted him. She had total and vivid recall of how angry he'd been when she'd said she'd believed he'd just tumbled out of Hester's bed! She could do without a repetition of that kind of scathing contempt, so she'd have to word her question carefully, keep it offhand, seemingly of no great importance.

The door was slightly ajar, and she pushed on it gently, her mind occupied with how she would bring in her question without making it apparent that she'd disturbed him expressly to do so.

The door swung open slowly, silently, not so much as a whisper from its well-oiled hinges, and her question was answered before it was asked.

Rafe was holding Hester in his arms, tenderly, lovingly. And his pain was written starkly on his face as he said levelly, his voice controlled, but darker, deeper than she remembered it, 'It's no use, Hester. No use at all. I *have* to marry Ziggy.'

That said it all, but if more were needed it was there in the tears that poured silently, despairingly from beneath Hester's closed eyelids as she clung to the man who was her lover, listening as he sorrowfully relinquished the woman he loved because it was his duty to make a marriage of expediency.

And as Ziggy turned away, too numb to do more than slip unheeded back to her room, her one coherent thought was that Hester, of all people, would understand the need to do one's duty.

CHAPTER ELEVEN

SHE WOULD go away, take her breaking heart with her. Broken hearts mended, she had to believe that. She couldn't put up with this kind of pain for ever.

It was not going to be easy. Gramps wouldn't be willing to see her walk away, but she'd cross that bridge when she came to it. Right now she was blindly staring out of one of Rafe's bedroom windows, hearing the noise of the shower from the adjoining bathroom.

She had thought long and hard and now it all added up, made sense of a kind. When she'd asked him why he wanted to marry her he'd said, Why do you think? It shouldn't be too difficult to work out. And knowing what she knew now it wasn't difficult at all, which should have warned her, but it hadn't. Rafe had asked her not to break the news until dinner—and now she knew why. He'd wanted to tell Hester first, break it to her gently, himself. Which was why he'd suggested she have a nap after lunch—to keep her out of the way, leaving the field clear for him to tell Hester, comfort her.

She'd thought long and hard about what she had to do, and she'd had the words lined up on her tongue when she'd tapped on his door before walking in. She'd called through the partly open bathroom door, 'It's me!' giving him fair warning because, above all, she wanted to be seen to be fair. It would counteract the murderous jealousy, the pain of losing love, that made her want to do something savage.

Like every other room at Staineswick, Rafe's bedroom was beautiful, but Ziggy took in none of the details. She knew only that the stamp of his personality was strongly here, surrounding her, permeating her skin, suffocating her.

She felt numb; the time for tears was not yet because she was going to have to play a part that would take all her acting ability. So far, her part in all this had been that of the fool, the painted clown, and now she had another role to play. The final role, because after she'd spoken to him the curtain would fall and they need never see each other again.

Her hands were clenched at her sides, her body rigid, the pain of loss almost too heavy to bear. She didn't know how she could have been so stupid. Why would a man like Rafe want to marry a girl like her? And the answer came back, as clear as crystal now that it had been thrust under her nose, the enormity of it unmissable. Because of her future part-ownership of Staineswick, that was why. No other reason.

Hester was the woman he loved, the one he would have chosen, had duty not intervened. Oh, he wasn't concerned about personal wealth, as she had once believed, she knew him well enough now to know that that was out. Rafe, in asking her to marry him, had the future welfare of Staineswick at heart. He could no more fall in love with her than fly. Fine clothes had made her fanciable, shown him she wouldn't disgrace her position as the future Lady Staineswick, but in his eyes she would always be a pain in the neck, outspoken, defiant, and, what was worse, the woman who had taken his beloved Hester's rightful place.

But it wouldn't come to that, of course. How could she marry him, knowing the truth? After tonight she would never see him again.

The noise of the shower ceased and her heart picked up its beat, pattering wildly. She couldn't imagine how she was going to go through with this, but she knew she had to, somehow.

She positioned herself carefully on the window seat, her tall, lithe body looking relaxed, hiding the inner turmoil that was pulling her apart. The bathroom door opened and Rafe was there, naked except for a towel hitched round his waist, his dark hair spiky, wet from the shower, his smile warm, his eyes warmer, just for her. But Ziggy knew he had to be putting on the act of his life, because she wasn't the woman he loved.

'Witch!' he said huskily. 'I'm already late changing for dinner, and you——' Laughter died in his throat and some other emotion took its place. He was probably remembering what had made him late. Hester would have taken a lot of comforting. Ziggy dropped her eyes because he looked magnificent, droplets of water glistening on the tanned sheen of his beautifully proportioned torso. And she loved him, and he loved Hester!

'I have to talk to you.' There was no way she could allow the farce to go on, to let him announce their engagement at dinner tonight, that would be intolerable. He hadn't seen her when she'd walked in on that pathos-filled love scene earlier. Her approach had been silent, not deliberately so, but silent all the same. And the lovers had been too absorbed in each other, in their grief, to have noticed her even if she'd marched right into the room, banging drums. So Rafe would have no reason to disbelieve what she was about to tell him.

'When I see you, talk is about the last thing on my mind,' he said with a sincerity that almost had her applauding his acting prowess. And he held out his arms to her—because this was part of the act? Or because she was fanciable? Or because he was desperate to find some way to push Hester to the back of his mind?

Ziggy didn't know, and she didn't care. She ignored the invitation, turning her back on him because she wouldn't be able to take the final humiliation—the look of relief, the gladness in his eyes, when he heard what she had to say.

'I've changed my mind,' she said, staring stonily through the window. There was ice in her voice, forcibly injected, to prevent any betraying wobble.

'About what?' Rafe sounded slightly amused, tolerant, and her spine stiffened with rejection of the whole charade.

'About us. Getting married. It would never work.' She achieved a slight shrug, closing her ears to the sound of his harshly drawn breath. She hurried on, before he started to try to get her to rethink—which he would feel he had to if she didn't get her say in first, 'You know me—I can't stomach being tied down to one place for long, and I guess that includes one man too. Sorry, Rafe, but there it is. We'd be good together in bed, I'll admit that, but what would happen when the novelty wore off and I started to get itchy feet?'

'I don't believe I'm hearing this.' Hard hands grasped her shoulders, snatching her round to face him, and his features were a hard mask, his mouth drawn and bitter. 'A few hours ago you said you loved me,' he ground out, his fingers hurting, the look in his eyes hurting more.

'So I made a mistake.' Ziggy moistened dry lips with the tip of her tongue, shaking inside but outwardly cool, detached. But she knew the mask of pain and anger would slip from his face when she played her final card. The joker in the pack. She closed her eyes because she didn't want to see it happen.

'I love Staineswick, believe it or not, but I don't want to get involved. Being committed to any place, or any one person, isn't my style. But I wouldn't want to see the estate suffer—I guess I'm too much of a Bellingham to want that.' Her eyes slid sideways, fixing on a gilt-framed picture on the wall because she couldn't bear the pain of looking at him.

'All I'm saying is——' she winced at the killing pressure of his hands '—that when the time comes—and I hope to heaven it isn't for ages—I'll sign over my share of the property to you. You can trust me in that, at least. And if you want to get your solicitor to draw up an undertaking to that effect, then I'll sign that too. And Rafe——' It was difficult to get his name out, becoming almost impossible to speak at all because of the bitter silence coming from him, 'that has to be between the two of us. I don't want Gramps hurt over something he can't change. Whatever I eventually inherit will go to you, for Staineswick. I do know how essential that is.'

'You've thought it all out, haven't you?' His tone was contemptuous as he drew her closer, savagely, and she couldn't stand that.

'Take your hands *off* me!' The words came out on a cry of pain and he released her at once, as if the contact burned, his dark eyes impaling her as he snapped,

'If that's what you want.'

'It is.' She snapped herself together. Somehow, she had to get out of this room. She was saying goodbye to the man she loved in the only way open to her.

With the entire Staineswick property safely in his hands he could marry Hester. She could safely leave the property that would come to her in Rafe's hands because she knew his stewardship would be good. She was releasing him from the emptiness of a marriage of convenience and he would thank her one day, probably already was, inside, but he wouldn't be crass enough to actually dance for joy, not while she was still in the room, so she left, her legs leaden, and she told him, 'I don't suppose we'll see each other again,' because she hoped that was the truth, and she knew he would want it that way too.

CHAPTER TWELVE

ZIGGY got the storm door closed behind her, struggling with the armload of Christmas gifts she'd bought that morning. This winter in Alberta had been particularly severe so far and would get worse before it got better, or so she'd been told.

Four carpeted steps led up to the kitchen, but she turned right, clattering down the stairs to the basement where she had her own room. From above her mother called out, 'Is that you, Zig? You have a visitor here,' and Aunt Connie added shrilly, 'Don't be long, now,' and they both sounded as pleased as Punch.

'Be right with you,' Ziggy called back, carrying on down. Her visitor could be any one of half a dozen people. She made friends easily and, since coming to live with her mother and aunt in Calgary, had made sure she didn't have time to brood, spending time with her friends when she wasn't working.

The nights were the worst, when Rafe, and what might have been if Hester hadn't been his real love, tormented her dreams.

She dropped her packages on her bed and got out of her heavy coat and boots, barely glancing in the mirror as she tweaked at her cord skirt and soft wool sweater, patted her hair which was braided round her neat head today. Sometimes she wondered if she should get it cut, a short, boyish style that would be easier to manage than this waist-length mane. But she never got around to it.

Her appearance had ceased to hold much interest for her since . . .

But she wouldn't think about that . . .

Idly wondering which of her friends had come calling, she crossed Jenny Oakes off her mental list. She had returned to Vancouver yesterday, after one of her flying visits. When Ziggy had returned to Canada, to stay with what was left of her family, she had contacted Jenny, determined to help the process of forgetting Rafe along with sheer hard work. It hadn't taken much doing to persuade Jenny that what they'd done in Vancouver they could do in Calgary, and the second domestic agency had been born.

Maybe her visitor was one of the team of women they hired? But she didn't think so. Everything had been running smoothly when she'd dropped by this morning, the newly appointed manageress had everything running like well-oiled clockwork.

She didn't know who to expect, and frankly didn't much care. But the one person she had never expected to see, ever again, was Rafe. But it was Rafe who rose from his chair as she walked into the living area. Rafe, whose presence filled the room, dragging the breath from her body.

The simmering tension that had always been between them, always there, even during their less fraught moments, filled the space, making her heart kick, making her aware of him as a potent force that had her weak with longing. She wanted him. Wanted him. And despised herself.

He had changed, she noted with wide, shocked eyes. He looked older, harder, leaner, and his smile was a grimace which didn't reach his eyes.

'There, isn't this a surprise!' Her mother made the understatement of the century and Aunt Connie, an older, slightly less pretty version of her sister Emily, chimed in,

'All the way from England—just to fetch you back for Christmas! What do you say to that?'

Nothing. Ziggy couldn't speak and she knew how it felt to be struck dumb. But not so Rafe. He had resumed his seat, his long legs stretched out in front of him, impeccably covered with the trousers of his dark grey suit, and his voice was impeccable too, the tone only very slightly dry.

'I think Ziggy's too stunned to say anything. Perhaps I should explain a little more fully?'

Aunt Connie fluttered her plump pink hands. 'Come along, Emily, we'll make a start on lunch, leave them to it,' but she paused in the doorway and wagged an arch finger. 'You're not to run away now, Rafe. There's no point in your staying elsewhere when we have a perfectly good guest room, is there, Emily?' Ziggy's mother agreed that no, there wasn't, and they wouldn't dream of letting him go, while Ziggy could have strangled her for looking as though a real live fairy story were being enacted before her very eyes.

Then they were alone and Ziggy turned hard, slanting eyes on him. 'What the hell are you doing here?' her voice betraying her distress, the distress she'd thought she had under control, except in her dreams. 'I never wanted to set eyes on you again!'

'I assure you, the feeling's mutual.' His eyes, granite-dark, outstared her and her own dropped, fastening on the clenched hands in her lap as if she'd never seen them before.

Rafe had changed. He'd been cold with her before, especially at the beginning of their stormy relationship. But this coldness was different, it went deeper. He was a hard-eyed, hard-faced stranger, who would hurt her as soon as look at her, and walk away without a backward thought.

'Then why are you here?' Her teeth snapped over the words. 'To get me to sign an undertaking to make my share of Staineswick over to you? Well, hand it over, I'd sign anything to see the back of you,' she said nastily, the pain of seeing him again, of knowing she still loved him, possibly always would, making her tongue acid. And he ground out, hatred in his eyes.

'Staineswick doesn't need you—never did. I have more than enough to plough into the estate, when the time comes, from my own enterprises, my own hard work. Taking anything from you is about the last thing I could stomach!'

Ziggy didn't try to make sense of his hateful words. They cut too deep and made her gesture of renunciation seem tawdry, worthless. And it hadn't been like that, and anger surfaced hotly. She wanted to strike him. Physical violence might ease the tension, but it wouldn't achieve a thing, not in the end, and her upper lip curled in derision as he said icily, 'I'm not here for my own pleasure, believe me, but for your grandfather's sake. I'm worried about the state of his health.'

'Oh, yes!' She wasn't buying that. 'The last time I heard from him, two days ago, he said he was fine.'

'He would, wouldn't he,' Rafe came back drily. 'And try to keep your voice down. We don't want those two patently nice and normal ladies through there to know we hate each other's guts.'

But I don't hate you! The unspoken words echoed through the corridors of Ziggy's mind. I still love you, dammit, and I wish to hell I didn't!

Rafe got to his feet, his features closed, making him a stranger, and with his back to her, he ostensibly interested himself in the cheap and tasteless ornaments spaced out along the shelf behind the sofa.

'Your grandfather's missing you,' he told her, his back view a telling portrayal of scorn. 'He's beginning to doubt your promise to return. Especially as your newsy little letters are full of this agency thing you've started. He's not a fool, Ziggy.'

That shook her. She felt bad about it, very bad, but what could she do? She should have known Gramps would see through her excuses.

During that last dreadful dinner at Staineswick, she had told him that she needed to go back to Canada, to see her mother, for one thing. She had talked as if she would be returning, bringing her mother for that visit he had talked about, but she had known that would never happen. She would never come back. It would be easier, so she had reasoned, to invent excuses for delaying her return once she was thousands of miles away. The launch of the new agency had been one of them, and in her latest letter to him she had hinted that an agency in Toronto was on the cards at some time in the not too distant future.

Rafe hadn't put in an appearance that last evening; Ziggy guessed he'd gone to see Hester to break the good news. Whatever, she had been thankful she hadn't had to share a table with him during what was to have been the happiest evening of her life so far and had turned out to be the worst.

Gramps and Léonie had been understanding about her wish to see her mother, but a little perplexed over her sudden decision. But Ziggy had insisted that she leave the next day, promising to write often. A promise she had kept because she missed them both, particularly her grandfather.

'There's nothing to be gained by my going back,' she told Rafe at last, her voice dull. She couldn't tell him she wouldn't be able to stand the sheer hell of seeing him every day, seeing him with Hester, and she tacked on, 'You know that.'

'I know nothing of the sort.' He swung round heavily, his mouth scornful. 'All I do know is you're a self-centred little bitch.'

His hands were bunched into the pockets of his trousers, his stance aggressive, and Ziggy shivered un-controllably, fighting tears.

How could he accuse her of being self-centred when she had renounced everything that was dear to her for his sake? Gramps, Staineswick, Rafe himself... If she hadn't witnessed that scene with Hester she wouldn't have known his true reasons for wanting to marry her. And if she hadn't known then maybe they could have had a good life together... That thought brought aching misery, and she pushed it away. A marriage between them would have been a disaster. Once the estate was secured he would have grown colder, more distant, finding solace from a union he had no heart for in Hester's more than willing arms. And that would have killed her.

But he didn't know any of that, and she couldn't tell him, and her head drooped forward, bowed down by emotional exhaustion, as icy words lashed her.

'He's pining for you—that's the long and short of it. I've been away in France since early July, but when I went to see him a week ago he looked a beaten man. It didn't take long to get the reason for the obvious decline out of him, and Léonie confirmed it. He's missing you, and more than that, he's convinced himself you won't go back. It's like the time your father walked out all over again. Only this time he can't take it. He's not a man in his prime now, he's old and he's frail and he can't take it.' Rafe swung on the balls of his feet, pacing the room, ending up directly in front of her.

'Look at me, Ziggy.' The command was unmistakable and tears spiked her lashes, turning the azure of her eyes to deepest sapphire. Her heart was bleeding for the old man who was being punished because she had foolishly fallen in love. He had been punished too much by those he loved and she wasn't going to add to his misery. She would have to go back, for a time at least, and Rafe told her, 'You're going back to Staineswick, like it or not. Your mother will go with you—I have seats booked on the afternoon flight out tomorrow afternoon. You will stay over Christmas and into the new year. It's his birthday at the end of January and you will be there for that because, the way he looks now, I doubt if he'll see another.'

At her muffled groan of protest, his warning tearing into her because, apart from Rafe, Gramps was the person she loved best in the world, he gave her a slow, disgusted look.

'Nothing moves you, does it? No one comes before your own selfish wishes. But protest as much as you like, it won't make one iota of difference. You're going to Staineswick, and there are two ways of doing it. You agree—no arguments or fuss, or I drag you on to that plane, kicking and screaming.'

Ziggy met his hard eyes, her own stormy. He would too. And if anyone questioned him he'd say she was nuts—and he'd be believed! He countered the violence in her eyes with a tight, meaningless smile.

'If it's any comfort to you, I won't be there. After delivering you to your grandfather I'll get out. I don't want to share space with you—you sicken me.'

But he covered his animosity with his own brand of urbane charm during lunch. The middle-aged sisters had gone to town over the meal. Normally, they had only a snack at midday, but today they'd produced wine and grilled halibut steaks. But Ziggy could hardly force the food down, Rafe's spurious but devastating charm, her mother's twittering, made her feel ill.

'I'm so excited I hardly know what I'm doing! Imagine—flying out tomorrow—meeting Ed's father at last!' Emily waved a fork in the air, her face crinkling with anticipation. 'Ed never spoke much about his family,' she told Rafe, leaning close and lowering her voice as if the walls had ears. 'And I had no idea his father was an earl—not until Ziggy wrote and told me she was visiting with him. She told me all about you too, young man!' Her mouth, as she lifted her wineglass, was coy, and Ziggy thought, not true. I wrote to you of his existence, but I didn't *tell* you anything, and she knew her mother was speculating on the fact that this savagely handsome, devastating and highly eligible man had flown the Atlantic to fetch her daughter. Rafe's face hardened briefly, as if he could read what was going on in that fluffy, faded blonde head, but his voice was light, pleasant enough, as he said,

'I'm sorry about the short notice, but I know Lord Staineswick is as anxious to meet you as he was to meet Ziggy.'

'Oh my!' Pink-cheeked, Emily flapped her hands in the air as if to lower her temperature, telling Rafe, 'The short notice doesn't bother me one bit, I'm raring to go,' then, appealing to her sister, 'Help me pick out some new clothes, Connie? We can ride into town this afternoon, visit the stores. I haven't a thing to wear that would be suitable for staying with an earl!'

And later, running Ziggy to earth in her basement, she said, 'I've shown Rafe to his room—the poor man must be jet-lagged. And you're going to have to see to his meal this evening. Connie and I won't be in. After we've finished downtown we'll take up that invite we had from the Goldings—just supper and bridge.'

It was the first Ziggy had heard of any such invitation and she guessed it was a spur-of-the-moment ploy to leave her alone with Rafe. And her suspicions were confirmed when her mother said casually, 'Isn't he gorgeous? I thought that when he came here before, asking your whereabouts, and I gave him your address in London. He said he was enquiring on your grandfather's behalf, but he didn't let on about the title and everything. And I just know he's fond of you—a mother can always tell.'

Which said very little for maternal intuition, Ziggy thought grimly as her mother rushed away, puffing as she took the basement stairs, in a hurry to go shopping for 'suitable' clothes. At one time Rafe had found her physically attractive, her future inheritance even more so, and had offered to marry her. But that was well and truly in the past. He hated the sight of her now, he'd said so.

She spent the afternoon packing. She didn't intend to take much, she'd left all the clothes she and Léonie had bought behind at Staineswick and she'd be able to renew her acquaintance with them. It would please Gramps, too, to see her wearing the things he'd provided.

Rafe's warnings about his health had worried her deeply and, knowing he was pining, she would have returned for a visit, even if she had known Rafe would be around. The fact that he wouldn't be was a bonus. It was his manner, his unforgiving attitude that had so hurt her. He hadn't needed to treat her like dirt to get her to return. He hadn't needed to come here, either, and threaten to drag her back like a prisoner under escort. A simple phone call explaining the state of Gramps' health would have been enough.

As the afternoon wore on the shock of seeing him again, the shattering pain of knowing she still loved him, translated itself, self-protectively, to anger.

Rafe had said he hated her, that she sickened him, and there was no call for that. No call at all. She had released him from a marriage commitment that must have irked him, to say the least, and had offered to make her future inheritance over to him. That he had told her he didn't want it wasn't relevant. So he should be licking her feet in gratitude! And what right had he to treat her like something contagious and nasty!

It was gone six when she heard him moving around overhead, and she faced the fact that she would have to feed the brute with less than graciousness. She had changed into a black jump-suit—black suited her mood—and, barefoot, as was her habit, she stumped up the basement stairs, at boiling point now. Grimly she told herself she'd feed him and leave him to spend the evening any way he chose. She might even look in on the Goldings' bridge party—and that would teach her mother a small lesson!

If Rafe treated her to any more verbal abuse—just one word!—she would stand up to him, let him feel the sharp edge of her tongue! It wasn't her fault that he hadn't gone ahead and married his obnoxious Hester. That he hadn't was obvious, because Léonie would have been full of the news in one or other of the many letters she had written.

So, if his love-life had gone sour on him, it wasn't her fault. She had done all she could in that direction—short of leading the pair of them to that altar!

'May I use your phone?' were the words that met her as she erupted into the kitchen. 'I'd like to let Dudley and Léonie know when to expect us.'

'Go ahead.' Ziggy deliberately didn't look at him, and the dismissive shrug that accompanied her words wasn't achieved without great effort. Her rage, already simmering, had almost boiled over at the sound of that smooth, superior voice!

She fetched a steak from the fridge and slapped it under the grill, clattering plates and cutlery to drown out the sound of his end of the telephoned conversation which was coming through from the living area.

Haphazardly, she set the table for one. No way was she sitting down to eat with him. Washed a salad, the tap at full bore, and shrieked, startled witless, as Rafe's hand came down on her shoulder.

'I think something's burning.'

'Hell!' Swallowing a few choicer expletives, she grabbed the grill pan and yanked over the smoking steak with a long-handled fork, then pattered back across the kitchen to turn off the gushing tap. While Rafe just stood there, watching, looking superior!

'Feeling flustered?' The sarcastic enquiry sent her temperature up several degrees, and he'd already seated himself at the table, his long legs sprawled out.

Ziggy made an elaborate detour around the obstruction to fetch a loaf from the wall cupboard, her temper only just under control, and dumped it, whole, on the table in front of him, then went to fish the drowned and half pulverized salad out of the sink.

'I might have known you'd be totally undomesticated,' Rafe commented hatefully. 'Your mother tells me,' he went on suavely, seemingly oblivious of her mounting fury, 'that you've become quite a changed person since your trip to England. Chastened, she said, though I can't see it myself. Less rumbustious. And, I quote, "So considerate of her poor old ma—as if the dear child's grown up all of a sudden." I never thought of you as being "rumbustious", though the word does fit your less civilised moods. I thought you were all sorts of things, though—self-opinionated, impossibly rude——'

'Must you snipe?' Ziggy was almost beside herself by now. She had had as much as she could stomach from him! Banging the charred piece of steak on to a plate, she took it over to him in a hand that wobbled with fury, and dumped it in front of him. 'Shut up, and eat!'

'What? That?' He looked pained and disdainful eyes rejected the offering, and Ziggy planted her hands on her slim hips and shrieked,

'Yes, buster—that! And I hope it chokes you!' Which wasn't very original but precisely summed up her feelings. Her flush was hectic, her eyes sparking with angry resentment. She hadn't meant to lose her temper with him, had meant to stay cool, keep her distance, but it was a relief to bawl him out, even though the sane little part remaining inside her head warned her that she might come to regret this outburst, become even more vulnerable because of it. But that part was ignored as she stormed on,

'You come into my home, acting like the king of some vastly superior race, and lay the law down to me! And— and treat me like rubbish—not fit to breathe the same air!'

She was truly furious with him and getting well into her stride. Hating him was better than loving him. Easier. And she had no intention of brooding over him ever again. Him! *Huh!*

'Finished?' Rafe enquired with a smooth hardness that would have done credit to iced water sliding over polished jet. Ziggy growled,

'Not by a long chalk! And eat your food. We're not affluent enough to waste good meat here! And if you don't like the way it's cooked,' she spat, recalling his insult about her lack of domesticity, 'what are you doing here, when you could be back home, having the suitable Hester cook you up an elegant little something? I dare say she cooks as perfectly as she does everything else!'

She made to turn away, to leave him to struggle with the inedible meat, but his voice stopped her, low and grim.

'*Who* did you say?'

Her lips curled scornfully and her slanting eyes mocked. 'Hester. You know—H.E.S.T.E.R.,' she spelled out. 'The so-suitable girl—*woman*,' she amended cattily, 'you're in love with.'

'Will you repeat that?' Rafe got up slowly, straddle-legged, his thumbs hooked into the waistband of his trousers. The attitude was casual, but there was nothing

casual about him at all. He looked like a man at the end
of his tether.

'You don't frighten me!' Ziggy voiced the self-assuring
words aloud, and just to prove it, pushed some more,
too far gone in her need to hold her own, to hurt before
he had the chance to hurt her any more, to realise precisely what she was saying.

'It's not my fault you're not already sharing a cosy
little love nest with her, married to the paragon at last.
I did my part to help things along. And all the thanks
I get is to hear you say you hate the sight of me!' At
that point her voice did shake, though she did her best
to hide it, clamping her mouth tightly shut. Only it hurt,
it really did, to recall those words, the naked dislike in
his eyes as he'd said them, and she missed the flicker of
something vital in those smoky eyes, heard only the tinge
of exasperation in the cool, smooth voice.

'Will you please tell me what you think you're talking
about?'

'What do you think?' Ziggy growled around the
treacherously betraying lump in her throat. 'And if that
doesn't satisfy you, tough! It's all you told me when I
once asked you why you wanted to marry me. Remember? And I worked it out—not quite by myself, I
needed a little help from you and Gramps.'

'I don't know what you're getting at,' Rafe's voice
was very quiet now, 'but did it ever occur to you that I
wanted to marry you because I loved you? That was what
I meant when I said it shouldn't be too difficult to work
out.'

She couldn't believe she was hearing this rubbish! She
had had the evidence of her own ears, her own eyes, to
tell her it was nowhere near the truth. She said distantly,
'No. No way,' and swung around, going through to the

living area, fumbling among the bottles on the drinks tray, pouring a stiff measure of vodka into a glass and topping it up with tonic.

'May I have one of those? I have the feeling I'm going to need it.'

'Help yourself.' Rafe had followed her, dammit, like Nemesis. And she couldn't take any more. Vitalising anger had drained out of her, leaving her limp and defeated in body and mind. 'I'm going to bed.'

'Not so fast.' Strong, ungiving fingers closed round her wrist and the touch of him, skin against skin and bone against bone, made her cry out with the mental pain of it,

'Let me *go*!'

'No. Not until we get to the bottom of the weird can of worms you've opened up tonight. And I'll sit up all night if I have to, and you'll sit right with me,' he warned. 'So start talking. What, precisely, did you mean me to "think"?'

Ziggy shrugged, weakly wanting to cry because his fingers had left her wrist. Her flesh, deprived of his touch, craved more. She wanted to cry because she was a fool, she had as good as divulged the thing she'd sworn she'd never to speak of. And he would know, without a doubt, that she hadn't refused to marry him because she didn't love him, refused to commit herself—and that would be the final ignominy.

'Well?'

She had slumped into an armchair and he stood over her, and she was too tired to try to fight any more. Sooner or later he'd have the truth out of her, so she might as well make it sooner, get it over with, creep into bed and cry herself to sleep, which was, after all, an exercise she was not unfamiliar with.

Swallowing her drink in one long gulp, she set the empty glass down on the arm of the chair, noticing, dispassionately, that her fingers were shaking. She dragged in a flustering breath and got it over with.

'On my last day at Staineswick, Gramps told me he'd been hoping you and I would marry because it would be the best thing out as far as the estate was concerned. And I got to wondering if he'd mentioned it to you, and if you'd agreed with him and saw marriage to me—so keeping the estate intact and in the same family—as the only way out.'

Even to her own ears her voice sounded dull. Flat. And Rafe wasn't helping, just standing, looking down at her, his expression saying nothing at all.

'So I decided to ask you,' she continued with a heaviness that echoed the beat of her heart. 'And when I found you, you were making love to Hester. She was crying. And you were telling her you *had* to marry me.' She shrugged, trying to achieve the unachievable, a semblance of uncaring uninterest—as if all this had happened a long time ago, had almost sunk beyond memory. 'It had to be for the sake of the estate—that much was obvious. There was no other reason on this earth why you should *have* to marry me. And that's about it. Except——' her lip curled in a final weak flare of temper '—that I did the decent thing. Released you from your dutiful need to marry for property rather than for love.'

There was a long, painful silence and she couldn't bring herself to look at him because she'd blown it now. She felt a clown, a sad clown, as she heard him move away, across the room, heard the clatter of glass against glass as he took more vodka. Then a single rough expletive, his voice grating with an emotion she couldn't put a name to.

Ziggy got unsteadily to her feet, a lifeless, hopeless puppet, and left him to his drink and his thoughts—whatever they were. He wasn't saying and she wasn't asking. She needed to be alone, to curl up under her duvet in a tight small ball. Her feet stumbled awkwardly at the foot of the basement stairs and she felt for her door, hands outstretched because tears were blinding her.

'Ziggy——' He had followed her down here, too, but it didn't seem to matter now. Nothing mattered. He knew all there was to know about her now. She only hoped he wouldn't gloat.

It was Rafe who opened her bedroom door, found the light switch, who steered her over to her bed, removed the suitcase she'd been packing earlier. She sank wearily down, rubbing her eyes with her knuckles.

'Did it ever occur to you that you might have been wrong?'

'About what?' She stared at the floor. He was sitting beside her on the bed, but she didn't turn to look at him. She couldn't. She had already revealed far too much.

'About Hester and me.'

'No.' Ziggy felt lightheaded. A stiff vodka—plus, she hadn't eaten all day—was taking its toll. 'Why should it? I always thought what a good couple you made. And I'd have been blind not to see how she worshipped you. And you seemed fond of her—a bit more than fond, sometimes. And you were making love to her that——'

'Correction.' A gentle finger was laid against her lips and her mouth trembled, her words dying in her throat. 'I was not making love to Hester, then or ever. I was trying to comfort her, which is an entirely different kettle of fish.'

'Fish?' she echoed stupidly, her slanting, tear-drenched eyes on him now. Rafe smiled, slow and sweet. He didn't look hard now, or hating, and his hands gently captured her face. 'I should put you over my knee and beat you for what you've done to us. Idiot!'

'Yes, I know.' It was the story of her life! But why, exactly, he should accuse her of being idiotic now she didn't know, not yet. And because he was close, so very close, and because the movement of his fingers as he brushed the tears from her face was too exquisite to be borne, she picked at his words, not understanding. 'Why should Hester need *comforting*?'

'It's a long story, and I should refuse to tell you any damn thing because you had the gall to believe I'd marry anyone for property. Good grief, woman, I could have kept Staineswick going on my own and hardly noticed a dent!' His hands left her face, almost pushing her away, and there was pain in his voice, bleak anger too, as he rasped, 'Dammit to hell, Ziggy! Do you realise what you've done?'

Bereft of words, of thought, even, she shook her head, and he grated right back at her, 'Then I'll tell you! You've put me through hell! Just tell me one thing,' his tone roughened. 'Did you ever love me? Even if only for a moment?'

'You know I did!' The words were torn from her before she could stop them, shadowed by only the smallest regret. Perhaps it was time they were honest with each other. Then his return to anger drained out of him, and there was a low sound in his throat as he reached out for her.

And she was there, for him, as she knew she would always be, as they kissed with the hunger of lovers who have been apart for too long, clinging to each other, their bodies, lips and hands asking questions, receiving answers, then Rafe said, a catch in his deep voice, 'Ziggy, I love you—how could you have done this to us?'

'I'm sorry. Sorry!' And she was, desperately, achingly sorry, and her face was wet with tears again. But happy tears, because she could hardly believe this was happening, that it wasn't a dream conjured out of her longing.

'Don't be.' He sounded calmer now, back in control, holding her close. 'People in love do the darnedest things. I read once that the state of being in love is close to insanity.'

Ziggy laughed softly, the sound shaken with tears, revelling in the joy of being in his arms, the sheer wonder of hearing his words of love, as he kissed her eyes, her lips, the end of her pointed chin, his mouth sliding down to her throat, and she heard the regret in his voice as he told her,

'I've practically grown up knowing Hester. I've been fond of her, like a brother, but never more than that.'

'You don't have to tell me,' she assured him gently, gloriously confident—confident enough to forget what she'd seen, but he raised his head, his eyes soft with love.

'I want to explain. I won't allow any cloud, no matter how insignificant, to shadow our marriage.'

Gently he pulled her down so that they were lying on the narrow bed, facing each other, very close.

'Unfortunately, Hester developed a crush on me. And I'll say this for her—she kept it well under control until you burst in on the scene. I think she knew how I felt about you before I knew myself.' His hand touched her cheek and she turned her head, putting a kiss in his palm, and she heard the intake of breath and closed her eyes because she still wasn't sure that this was happening.

'She had come to my office that day and, to put it politely, began to make advances,' Rafe told her. 'They were too blatant to ignore, or laugh off, so I did the only thing I could, I told her that you and I were to be married. She started to cry then, and I was sorry for her. I felt humble in a way because you had just made me so happy, and she was so very unhappy. She kept saying over and over that I couldn't marry you. That you would never love me as she did. Stuff like that.' He shrugged, and it was the first time Ziggy had ever seen him embarrassed. She smiled, loving him ... Loving him!

'So—well, heck, Ziggy! I didn't quite know what to do with her. She was hysterical by that time. She'd started to yell—so I slapped her, just once. It had to be done, and it worked. She calmed down. Just cried, quietly.'

'Then you held her in your arms because you were sorry you'd had to slap her,' Ziggy supplied, knowing just how he would have reacted, and why.

'Yes.' The blunt affirmative was touched by pain. 'And if you'd stayed around to listen you would have heard me telling her that I had to marry you because you were the only woman on this earth who could make me whole, complete, happy. That I needed you as I need air to breathe.'

'And I ruined everything,' Ziggy said reflectively, miserably. 'What a fool I was!'

'Exactly,' Rafe agreed, his mouth finding hers. 'A fool. But then so was I. I was too ready to accept your story of being incapable of a lasting relationship. But your independence had been one of the first things I'd admired about you, and I took it for granted that you were telling me the truth—that your independent spirit wouldn't let you tie yourself down. I should have made you tell me the whole story—that you were trying to give me my freedom. That was the way you saw it, wasn't it?'

'Precisely,' Ziggy murmured softly against his lips, weak with the invasion of need for him. Rafe moved closer,

'You didn't ruin anything that can't be mended, my dear love. And right now,' his arms gathered her to the warmth of him, 'right now I intend doing a pretty thorough repair job.'

'Lovely!' Her arms went round him and she wriggled closer, twining her legs around the length of his, and before all hope of coherent thought was blotted out, she whispered,

'Did Gramps ever tell *you* he wanted us to marry to hold the estate together?' quite unprepared for the husky laughter that spread warmth and deep contentment through her.

'He wouldn't have dared! He knows I'm a man who makes his own mind up. And I made mine up about you after the first time I kissed you, when I saw how genuinely upset you were when you thought he was ill. And talking of your grandfather,' his hand dealt with the zipper of her jump-suit and his voice faltered, thickening with desire as he gazed down at her exposed, perfect breasts, 'our marriage—and you are going to marry me,' his tone brooked no argument, none at all, 'is going to make him one very happy person.'

'So that will make three of us. Five, if we count in Léonie and Mum,' Ziggy sighed blissfully, wriggling closer. 'Kiss me, Rafe. I don't want any more talk, not for hours!'

And, devotedly, he did just that.

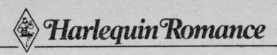 **Harlequin Romance**

Coming Next Month

#2965   NO GREATER JOY   Rosemary Carter
Alison fights hard against her attraction to Clint, driven by
bitter memories of a past betrayal. However, handsome,
confident, wealthy Clint Demaine isn't a man to take no for
an answer.

#2966   A BUSINESS ARRANGEMENT   Kate Denton
When Lauren advertises for a husband interested in a businesslike approach to marriage, she doesn't expect a proposal from a
handsome Dallas attorney. If only love were part of the
bargain....

#2967   THE LATIMORE BRIDE   Emma Goldrick
Mattie Latimore expects problems—supervising a lengthy
engineering project in the Sudan is going to be a daunting
experience. Yet heat, desert and hostile African tribes are
nothing compared to the challenge of Ryan Quinn. (More about
the Latimore family introduced in THE ROAD and TEMPERED
BY FIRE.)

#2968   MODEL FOR LOVE   Rosemary Hammond
Felicia doesn't want to get involved with handsome financial
wizard Adam St. John—he reminds her of the man who once
broke her heart. So she's leery of asking him to let her sculpt
him—it might just be playing with fire!

#2969   CENTREFOLD   Valerie Parv
Helping her twin sister out of a tight spot seems no big deal to
Danni—until she learns she's supposed to deceive
Rowan Traynor, her sister's boyfriend. When he discovers the
switch his reaction is a complete surprise to Danni....

#2970   THAT DEAR PERFECTION   Alison York
A half share in a Welsh perfume factory is a far cry from Sophie's
usual job as a model, but she looks on it as an exciting
challenge. It is unfortunate that Ben Ross, her new partner,
looks on Sophie as a gold digger.

Available in March wherever paperback books are sold, or
through Harlequin Reader Service:

In the U.S.
901 Fuhrmann Blvd.
P.O. Box 1397
Buffalo, N.Y. 14240-1397

In Canada
P.O. Box 603
Fort Erie, Ontario
L2A 5X3

ATTRACTIVE, SPACE SAVING BOOK RACK

Display your most prized novels on this handsome and sturdy book rack. The hand-rubbed walnut finish will blend into your library decor with quiet elegance, providing a practical organizer for your favorite hard-or soft-covered books.

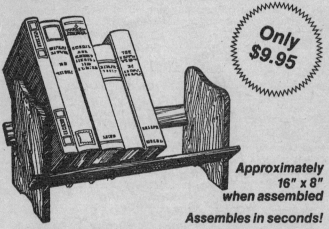

Only $9.95

Approximately 16" x 8" when assembled

Assembles in seconds!

To order, rush your name, address and zip code, along with a check or money order for $10.70* ($9.95 plus 75¢ postage and handling) payable to *Harlequin Reader Service*:

Harlequin Reader Service
Book Rack Offer
901 Fuhrmann Blvd.
P.O. Box 1396
Buffalo, NY 14269-1396

Offer not available in Canada.

BKR-1A

*New York and Iowa residents add appropriate sales tax.

Keepsake